CHRISTMAS at *Sonshine Barn*

Mayo Love Story

❆

Sarah Soon

Christmas at Sonshine Barn
Copyright © 2023 by Sarah Soon
Published by Write by Grace, LLC

All rights reserved.

No part of this publication may be reproduced, distributed, or transmitted in any form or by any means, including photocopying, recording, or other electronic or mechanical methods, without the prior written permission of the publisher, except as permitted by U.S. copyright law.

This is a work of fiction. Names, characters, places, and incidents are the product of the author's imagination or are used fictitiously. No resemblance to persons (living or deceased), actual events, locales, or products is coincidental.

Library of Congress Cataloging-in-Publication Data
Names: Soon, Sarah, author
Title: Christmas at Sonshine Barn
Description: Tulsa: Write by Grace, LLC, 2023

Identifiers:
ISBN: 979-8-9879644-2-2 (hardcover)
979-8-9879644-0-8 (ebook)
979-8-9879644-1-5 (paperback)

Book Cover Photography by Sarah Freeman
Book Cover Design by 100 Covers
Book Interior by 100 Covers
Edited by Two Birds Author Services

Table of Contents

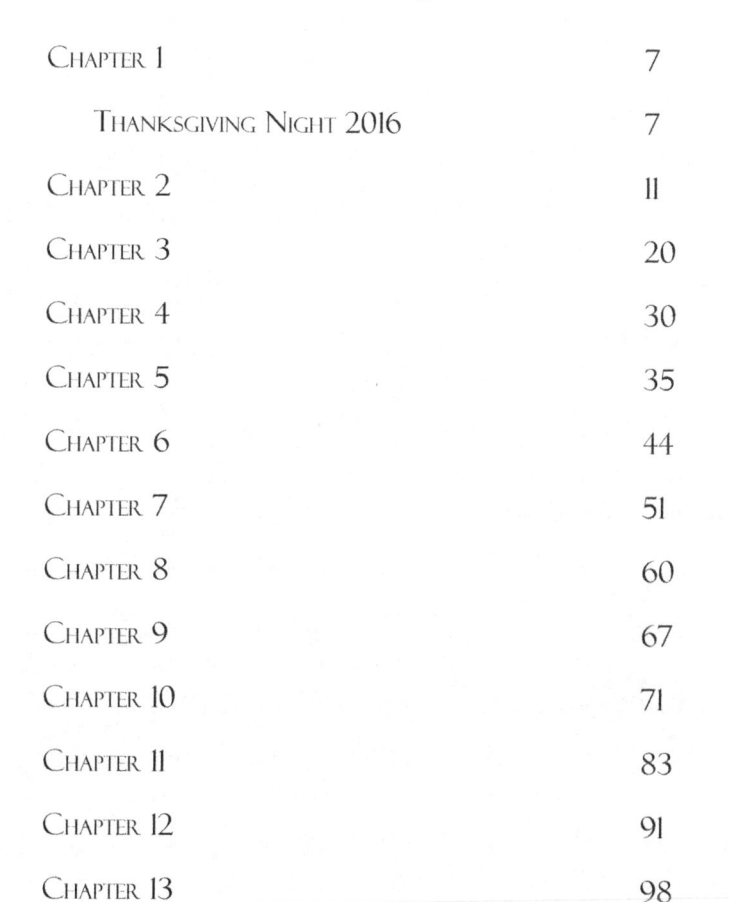

CHAPTER 1	7
THANKSGIVING NIGHT 2016	7
CHAPTER 2	11
CHAPTER 3	20
CHAPTER 4	30
CHAPTER 5	35
CHAPTER 6	44
CHAPTER 7	51
CHAPTER 8	60
CHAPTER 9	67
CHAPTER 10	71
CHAPTER 11	83
CHAPTER 12	91
CHAPTER 13	98
CHAPTER 14	108
CHAPTER 15	115
CHAPTER 16	124

Chapter 17	132
Chapter 18	141
Chapter 19	150
Christmas Eve	150
Chapter 20	159
Christmas	159
Chapter 21	163
Chapter 22	169
Chapter 23	176
Chapter 24	183
Chapter 25	187
New Year's Eve night	187
A Letter from the Author:	197
Excerpt	199
Acknowledgements	209
About the Author	211

I dedicate this book to my parents, Denny and Sandy Freeman, for supporting my dream to write. And of course, for starting the venue, Sonshine Barn Wedding and Event Center.

And to my husband for your unconditional love and support.

Chapter 1
Thanksgiving Night 2016

It was a long time coming. After seven months of dating my "It" girl, I was engaged, two months shy of my thirty-first birthday. Earlier tonight, my proposal went smoothly, and now I was ready to sleep.

I turned on my sound machine since it drowned out urban noise and helped me relax, playing a symphony of wildlife from courting cicadas, whistling nightingales, and a trickling river.

I recited the Lord's Prayer like I do every night. "Our Father who art in Heaven..." Then, when I got to: "Your will be done—"

A flash of white light illuminated the darkness. How could lightning hit without a storm? Before I could investigate, a young woman in a cherry-red, off-the-shoulder gown appeared. A golden haze shrouded her face. Her flowing blonde hair fanned in all directions like gilded lupines in the wind. Her slender arms extended toward me, and I catapulted upright.

On her wrist was... Granny Mason's bracelet. Four-strand Akoya pearls and a yellow gold clasp of emeralds, sapphires, citrines, rubies, and diamonds. I reached out to grab the heirloom, but I clutched only air. Who was she?

I stood, bare feet touching the sheepskin rug. I turned on the lamp and turned off the sound machine. I was alone. The reclaimed oak floors showed no ghostly impressions of footsteps. The blackout forest-green shades were still pulled down. Everything was in its place. No projectors streamed from outside, not that I'd expect anyone to prank me at this age; my former frat brothers were too domesticated now as they tucked their kids into bed, kissed their wives good night, and fell sound asleep.

Yet my solitude didn't slow my heightened pulse. The last time I experienced a vision, I was in addiction recovery at a rehab center. A white light had filled the room but disappeared within seconds. As of tonight, I'd been sober for years, so I didn't have an explanation. That disturbed me.

I sauntered to the living room, turning on the picture light above a 11x14 gilded framed photograph I had taken of Granny. Donned in an emerald-green gown, she sat on her wingback chair. The bracelet on her white gloves added a layer of color and texture. She gifted this picture to Gramps for their sixtieth wedding anniversary.

I touched the glass as if I could grab the bracelet. I hadn't seen the heirloom for five years (shortly after Granny died) since I kept it at my parents' *for now*. The bracelet embodied Granny, so I didn't want it with me, afraid I'd miss her too much.

Every anniversary, Gramps bragged about how he stole Granny's heart from her rich beau. How Gramps got drafted to fight the bastard Nazis while her steady paid someone off, so he could stay home. Gramps wrote Granny almost every day. When he returned from war, he drained his savings to commission the bracelet to seal the deal. Granny would pipe up, saying through his letters, she fell in love. What I'd do to hear them tell that story again.

"You would've loved Pres. She's classy, poised, and beautiful, like you. I wish you could attend our wedding."

It hit me. Pres could wear it for her "something borrowed", incorporating Granny. I winked at "Granny," thanking her for the "tip."

I sat on the sectional near the picture, and I rested my head on the padded back. Within a few minutes, my eyes closed, and I drifted off to sleep.

My phone playing Pres's ring tone woke me up. Was she okay? I sprinted to the bedroom where it charged on the nightstand.

"Hey, what's going on?" I asked, squeezing the phone tight.

"I can't sleep." To my relief, she was upbeat. This night took me on a wilder emotional ride than alcohol ever did. "My mind's buzzing about wedding planning. When were you thinking we should marry? Maybe in a year?"

I should've known. An obsessive planner, Pres scheduled life a week, a month, a quarter at a time, so I never winged a date, but gave her at least a few days' notice. Now, I hesitated to spring this summer on her, but I couldn't endure a long engagement.

"Are you there?" she asked.

"Let's look at July when I book my vacation." I cleared my throat, hoping she'd run with it, just this once.

"But that only gives us eight months."

"That's plenty of time, especially for an intimate wedding."

"If a guest list of two hundred and fifty is small, I'm all for it, but anything less risks omitting close friends. But let's consider this July..." Her voice trailed off; she must be upset or stressed. Once something was planned, she marched onward to the frontlines.

"Our families will help." I sat on the edge of the bed, fighting frustration and fatigue.

"You say that, but how will we wedding plan in Michigan? We'll be spending all that time with your family—"

"You're on overload. Let's get some sleep and then talk about all things wedding on Monday."

We both had Mondays off.

"Trust me, I want to bask in the glow of our engagement, but if we want a summer wedding, we must plan now. The holidays are peak engagement times. We need to secure a date, a venue, and vendors immediately." She gave orders like a coach on the sidelines.

I looked on top of the dresser at a 5x7 photo of my family. Mom would want to offer input on the venue. "Let's talk to our families first."

"But they'll support whatever decisions we make."

"Like I said..." I exhaled so I wouldn't lose my cool. "Let's talk on Monday."

"You're right. I better get to sleep. I love you and can't wait to be your wife!"

"Love you too." After I hung up the phone, I reached into my nightstand drawer and grabbed a chocolate bar. Thank God, we only had eight months until we'd marry.

Chapter 2

On my day off, I wanted to edit the engagement photos from the proposal, so for easier viewing, I tethered my laptop to the TV. Lauren, my sister, took them with my personal camera while her husband, Shane, shot the video. Each image told the night's story.

After the Thanksgiving feast, we moved to my parents' living room. I had focused so much energy on popping the question, I struggled to carry a conversation or notice anything beyond Pres and me. Lauren captured me running my hands through my hair, wiping sweat on my pants, and staring off into space. How did I get through the night? I enjoyed reliving it now since the photos helped me to see what I had missed.

In most of the pictures, our families didn't interact much. My side sat on the right section of the room, Pres's on the left, while we were in the middle, establishing a neutral zone. Of course, Dad talked to each side, trying to unify everyone. But I wasn't concerned since we'd get better acquainted over time. Holidays, kids, and vacations would bring us together.

And there was the shirt fiasco. I had to change into Dad's overly tight, bright-colored polo since I'd perspired through my comfortable grey V-neck. I didn't expect my insides to get twisted into a pretzel before I got on one knee. I've shot other couples' proposals, so I assumed mine would be straightforward.

Now, here was a terrific picture: I grabbed Pres's hand (she looked smokin' in her black leggings and cream off-the-shoulder top). After a short tribute about how grateful I was that God brought us together, I debated if I needed to kneel on my right or left leg. But after a few seconds, I got on my right, opened the ring box, and sprang the question.

She covered her mouth and hugged my neck. Before I could slip the ring on her finger, I dropped it. Lauren captured me on my knees frantically searching and finding it underneath the armchair. After I slipped it on Pres's finger, we kissed. I'd frame that image and hang it in my bedroom.

Grandpa Bettencourt approached with a Cuban cigar and an "attaboy," like a rite of passage. Finally, I wouldn't be his only single grandchild. Our families encircled us, and her dad prayed a blessing. I'd print that shot and gift it to our parents.

In the next picture, Mom was scowling. Why? She stood behind me, hands on my shoulders, lips pursed, and brows furled like I was late for dinner. She was probably tired from cooking most of the feast.

The doorbell rang. Pres entered, her arms loaded with her black satchel, cream purse, and two drinks.

"Hi, baby," I said, taking the drink carriers from her.

"I picked up smoothies for lunch. I've got to get in bridal shape, so I'm watching my calories."

I placed the drinks on the dining room table, and then she approached. I wrapped my arm around her small waist. She was perfect, but I'd have to remind her. How many times did I encourage brides at a photo session or at the wedding, they were beautiful?

"You're perfect." I drew her into a bear hug.

"Thanks." She gave me a kiss. "But I want to get fit. I'm hitting the gym at least five days a week."

"You can run with me."

She stuck her tongue out. "I hate running. I'll take group classes like HIIT, spin, and yoga."

She moved my pile of keys, receipts, and loose change off the dining table and placed them neatly into a wicker basket on top of my buffet server. She wiped the table clean and sat. "Why don't you sit next to me? We've got a lot of topics to cover."

"What kind did you get me?" I asked, sitting in the chair.

"Chocolate peanut butter sweetened with Stevia. Mine's a strawberry pineapple." She took a sip of her drink.

I tried mine. Not bad, but I didn't like the sweet aftertaste.

"Before we dive into wedding planning, I've got to get something off my chest." She set the drink hard on the table. "You need to know that your mom disrespected Dad."

I hung my head, wondering what Mom said. "What happened?"

"On Thanksgiving, Dad shared with her how they're opening new satellite campuses and adding more conferences. So, they need a gifted photographer like you in their media department."

"Yeah, I told him I'd be up for helping. That's when Mom approached. You called me over, so I didn't hear their conversation."

"Your mom rebuked him, saying you're too talented to get stuck working for a church. It'd be like hiring Billy Graham as a staff evangelist." I cringed. When it came to her kids, Mom didn't hold back.

"I'm sorry she disrespected him." I rubbed my forehead. A mild headache formed.

"Thanks for seeing that. She acted as though Dad's church is this homespun community and not a potential megachurch."

"You shouldn't assume. She was defending me more than considering the church." My throat tightened as I realized how little time our families spent with each other. Thank God we had a lifetime of getting acquainted and ironing out these minor issues.

"I understand you defending her." Pres took my hands in hers. "But since we're going to be a family, we need to address issues immediately. Otherwise, problems will accelerate."

I couldn't let this happen. I expected that becoming engaged would resolve my single issues and my family's enthusiasm to see me married. Instead, it sprouted new challenges. Still, these struggles were worth facing. "I'll talk to her." I kissed her on the forehead.

"Appreciate it, babe." She released her hands and took a sip of her smoothie. "I talked to Cheryl on my way here. I'm—"

"Who's she?" I'd have to slow her down as she switched gears faster than a Formula One driver.

"My friend in Vegas. She's a wedding planner and will help plan my wedding."

"Our wedding." I might have to remind her several times.

"Of course, it's our wedding." She waved her hands. "Anyway, she works for this high-end agency, but will give us a deal on her fees. What do you think?"

I scowled as confusion replaced chaos. "Can she plan our Tulsa wedding?" When I shot weddings, I'd get inspiration for backdrops and landscapes. Very different from women daydreaming about their weddings ever since they were girls.

Pres grabbed a large cream planner from her satchel hanging on the back of a spare chair. "That's what I wanted to discuss."

"Did you buy a new planner?" I asked.

She always carried one, while I preferred using apps on my phone. One less item to lug around.

"Mom gifted it for wedding planning. Isn't it cute?" She set it on the table.

I didn't care as long as it made her life easier. "Sure."

"Cheryl has so many brilliant ideas."

"Like what?"

She paused then grabbed a black fountain pen and tapped the barrel's end on the table. Uh-oh... she was about to drop a bomb.

"Pres?"

She smiled. "Vegas is the wedding capital of the world."

I tugged at my shirt collar and frowned.

"What's that look?" she asked.

"What?" I released my hand.

She sat on the side of the chair, squarely facing me. "Like you've lost your best friend."

I wanted to say I knew what would look best for pictures, but I took the more diplomatic route. "I assumed we'd marry outside, in a garden, the woods, or on a hill. The desert isn't exactly what I had in mind."

"How about we have an outdoor reception in Tulsa?" She patted my knee.

"Maybe, but we have time to decide." I didn't want to back down.

"Not really. Eight months isn't much time and until we settle on a venue, we're at a standstill."

"I see. Let's discuss other issues first." I needed to buy time.

"Alright." She opened her planner. Of course, it was specifically for weddings.

"We'll hire Philip, my second shooter, and I'll ask Shane for a referral for a videographer," I said.

"Great, but we need two of each."

I smiled, relieved we agreed on something. "Of course. So, cross those vendors off your list."

She turned to a page-long "Vendor" checklist. Check, check. Hopefully, she didn't expect us to decide all the vendors today.

She turned to a bookmarked page and frowned.

"What's going on?" I asked.

"It's—" She turned away. She was on "The Ceremony Venue" page.

My phone rang.

"Do you need to answer that?" Pres said.

"Mom can wait."

"Please answer her and set up a time to talk." She pointed to my phone.

"Only after we address what's going on with you."

She turned to me, eyes misty. "I've dreamt of marrying in Dad's church since I was a little girl."

"Oh." My insistence on an outside wedding began weakening.

"Since my brothers didn't marry there, it'd mean the world to him if we did." She clapped. "I've got it! How about you and your family plan the Tulsa reception, and you plan our honeymoon? We can spend it exploring nature and the beach."

I could pacify Mom if I delegated some of the planning for the reception to her while I focused on the honeymoon. I wanted the beach and the mountains. Lay out one day and hike the next. "I can get on board with that. Can I surprise you with our honeymoon destination?" I narrowed my gaze. That would be the only way I could plan without her intervention.

"Baby." She threw her arms in the air. "You know how I loathe surprises. At least tell me, and I won't change anything."

I raised my brows, unsure if she could stay neutral. "I'll hold you to that promise."

She hugged me. After we separated, she grabbed her phone from the satchel. "I'm going to call Cheryl. She'll want to start right away." She pointed her phone at me. "Why don't you call your mom now?"

My heart sunk. I wasn't in the right headspace to confront her, especially since I just surrendered my vision for an outside ceremony. "Fine." I stood and went to the patio.

Mom answered immediately. "Your dad and I talked and wanted to discuss your wedding." Her tone was upbeat. Organizing people and events was her superpower. "What about getting married at the Philbrook Gardens? I only mention this now because if that'll work for you two, you want to book it today."

"About that..." I didn't want to drop the bomb now, yet I needed to pacify both women. "Pres is here, so I'll let you know. I was calling to set up a time to discuss planning, so how about I come over this week?"

"Tomorrow?"

"No, Moriah's coming to work, but my Wednesday afternoon is free."

"How about you join us for dinner?"

"Great."

After I hung up, I walked inside. I stopped at the threshold of the dining room and watched Pres. She threw her head back, laughing. I loved her passion and energy. So, what was one day compared to a lifetime together?

She waved me over. "Wait until I tell Garrett," she said in a high-pitched tone. "Oh, my gosh! I love the way you think." I joined her at the table. "He's here now. I'm putting you on speaker."

"Sounds good." The female voice matched Pres's tone and excitement; it was like stumbling into a sorority meeting.

"Gar, this is my friend and our wedding planner, Cheryl."

"Hi, Cheryl. You got my girl excited."

"Nice to meet you. I'd say it's you who've put the joy back into Presleigh's step. Anyway, we were talking about how perfect it'd be to submit your photos to a wedding magazine. It'd be free advertising for your business since we're hiring your shooter and highlighting Pres's church."

"That's something to consider, but we can wait on that, right?" If Moriah were here, she'd be telling Cheryl, "Of course!" But I knew what submitting photos for publication meant—a high-end wedding. Nothing like the intimate, low-key affair I wanted.

"We need to make sure it's unique and visually appealing. A black-tie affair with guests wearing black, Pres and her bridal party wearing cream, and you and your groomsmen in black. The monochromatic theme is just catching on, so we'd be at the front of the trend." Cheryl's assertive tone irritated me. I was a client not her assistant.

"I'd prefer color. Blues here and there. Let guests choose between black, cream, or blue, so it still looks clean." I needed to rein her in before she casted my vision aside. Plus, I was worried my family wouldn't approve, especially Mom, who wore bright colors throughout the year. I didn't want my family left out.

"Babe," Pres said, "let the expert decide. We'll have a garden theme for our Tulsa reception. Let it explode with color if it'd make you happy."

"I'm an expert myself, so I know what color scheme will stand out." I was curt as Pres discounted my wedding experience.

"As a photographer, you know how sharp that monochromatic look is," Cheryl said. "And I haven't planned an all-black-and-white wedding yet, which is why I know it'll capture those magazines' attention. They prefer to feature emerging trends."

"Let me think about it." I didn't like being cornered.

"Cheryl, I'll let you know once we decide," Pres said.

"If you two can fly out here next week—I know it's short notice, but eight months is a tight window—we can secure a reception venue, baker, and a florist."

"What a great idea! I could get my bridal gown then. Won't Mom be excited? Could you schedule an appointment with MaidenWhite?"

"Of course. I don't mind pulling a few favors for you... If you'll excuse me, I've got to head to a meeting. I'll call you after. Nice to meet you, Garrett. I look forward to seeing you next week."

"Thanks Cheryl," I said.

She reminded me of some of the more assertive wedding planners I've worked with. I knew how to maneuver through their demands.

"Bye," Pres said then hung up. "I better get us plane tickets. Call Mom. Ask the woman's pastor if I can take the week off—"

I touched her arm. "I'm sorry, baby, but I can't make it. Next week, I have a meeting and two gigs."

"Can't you reschedule them?" She tilted her head to persuade me.

Irritated, I released my hand. "I might be able to reschedule the meeting with the potential bride. But I have a photo shoot at a wedding venue, and I'm covering a bridal shower."

"When is the shoot?" She flipped to the calendar page of her new planner.

"Wednesday."

"We could go from Sunday to Tuesday. At least we could decide on a reception venue."

I shook my head. "The bridal shower is on Sunday."

"Can Philip cover for you?"

"When I said I couldn't go, I meant it. He'll be out of town."

"Alright then." She slammed her planner shut. "I'll ask Moriah. And we'll have to FaceTime when I'm meeting vendors."

"That'll work. Oh, are you going to ask Lauren?"

"To come to Vegas?" She raised her brows.

"That, and if she'd serve as a bridesmaid." Lauren was as extroverted, fashionable, and jovial as Pres. They'd bond as tight as twins.

Pres's shoulders slumped. "I doubt she can get the time off, but yes, about the latter."

"What's wrong?"

She frowned. "I didn't want to say anything, but sometimes she treats me like I'm a teenager. I get that she's nine years older, but our age difference doesn't matter anymore."

My stomach tightened at these family "weeds." I'd better deadhead them now.

"Tell it to her straight. She'll listen." I caressed her back, hoping it'd reassure her.

"K... Will you be upset if I don't ask her to come to Vegas?"

"No. She'll be happy serving as a bridesmaid."

"Thanks." She gave me a peck on the cheek. "Oh, I almost forgot. What did your mom say?"

"I didn't bring it up, but I'll address it on Wednesday."

"K..."

My shoulders slumped. "What?"

"I don't want you to procrastinate."

"I get that. It's why I told you I'm talking to her on Wednesday."

"You don't have to be curt."

"I'm sorry, but everything's happening so fast." If only we could elope to the woods or the mountains. A man could dream.

"Buckle your seat belt, babe, because if you want to marry this summer, this is how it's going to be." She tapped my chest.

"I'll get on board, but with one caveat."

"What?"

"We don't discuss wedding planning on Mondays, so we can focus on us." I caressed her cheek.

"That's a great idea. Dad always counsels couples that a wedding is a moment in time, while marriage is for life." She grabbed my wrist, freezing my hand in place.

"Wise statement."

After Pres left, all I could think about was ironing things out with Mom. I might not survive this wedding.

Chapter 3

My mom and I had a complicated relationship. I loved her but I struggled with her control. When I'd confront her, she'd become defensive, justifying herself by saying that she was only helping. What a word, help. It could signify providing aid to someone in need, but that was it. I didn't need her unsolicited advice. When I did, I'd ask.

I usually ignored the dynamic until a specific problem arose. Perhaps not the best strategy, but I couldn't see a way forward.

So, when I drove to their house Wednesday afternoon, I played a mental tug of war: get her to apologize to Pres's dad, be congenial about a Vegas wedding, and represent my vision for a Tulsa reception. Every scenario warred with her fear of losing me or her not getting the vision she wanted.

On their front porch, Mom decorated the railings with lighted garland. Big gold ball ornaments adorned the doorposts, and a wreath with a large red bow hung in the middle of the door. Two black topiaries with lighted mini firs guarded each side of the entrance. Mom worked hard at creating a photogenic home, worthy of a spread in *Southern Living*.

I preferred something more rustic like my front porch. I decorated with lighted deer, a wooden sleigh, and a small pile of faux birch logs.

Mom answered the door. "Thanks for coming over. How are you?" she asked.

Did she want the truth or a courtesy statement? It was best to start slow. "Good," I said.

She closed the door. "Dad's grilling, so we can chat. Are you two wedding planning yet?"

"We're working with a planner and probably will have half our vendors booked by the end of the week." I removed my jacket.

"Here, I'll take that," she said. Then she put my jacket in the closet in the front entry.

I grabbed an orange and green candy cane from a ceramic bowl on the glass table.

I followed her into the living room off the entry. Red bows covered two wingback chairs, which Pres and I occupied on the night of the proposal. Red velvet ribbon, pliers, green twist ties, and gold storage boxes labeled *Christmas Decorations* covered the hardwood floor. An artificial Christmas tree strewn with white lights stood in the left corner.

I craned my neck, looking beyond the tree, to see Dad outside. On the spacious deck, he stood over the grill, staying warm in a thermal jacket and a wool hat.

Mom decorated for every season, and for Christmas, she started on Black Friday. She'd put the live tree in the living room and place smaller artificial ones in every room. She didn't stop until she finished transforming the house into a Christmas village, with garland, poinsettias, and candles, just like Granny.

The love for Christmas ran deep in my family. Every year, I got a live tree and decorated it with nature ornaments. This year though, she bought the faux tree since we would be celebrating Christmas in Michigan. And I skipped the tree altogether for the same reason, although I was bummed I wouldn't enjoy the pine scent filling my living room. But experiencing a white Christmas would be worth the sacrifice.

"How about some wassail?" Mom touched my shoulder.

"Sure."

She warmed the seasonal brew in a large slow cooker. An aroma of cider, cinnamon, and citrus wafted, inciting memories of Granny and me making the punch. I'd prep the apples, oranges, and pineapples for juicing since she insisted the secret was using fresh fruit. When she taught me how to whip the egg yolks into a froth, it wasn't long until I could form stiff peaks rivaling the waves of the Pacific.

"Have you two decided on a date?" Mom poured wassail into a white Christmas mug painted with an illustration of a gold ornament.

"July eighth."

"You should contact the Philbrook today and check if that date is available." Mom handed me the mug.

I might as well rip off the Band-Aid. "We're marrying in Vegas." I winced.

I caught the mug just as she dropped it. Some frothy foam dripped onto my hand. She grabbed a paper towel and wiped my hand dry. "Sorry about spilling it, but I think I got it all."

"No problem."

She frowned. "You *loathe* Vegas."

"It's Pres's wish since her brothers didn't marry at their dad's church." I took a sip of the sweet drink to counteract her sour reaction.

"Is that her dad's idea? He wouldn't stop bragging about his church. How they're opening a new campus. How he hired a dynamic youth pastor. On and on. He acted like you two were moving there." Mom tossed the paper towel in the trash bin.

That was my cue. "Hey, did you tell her dad I was overly qualified to shoot photos for his church?"

Mom lifted her chin. "I sure did. He wanted to stifle your creativity and waste your talent in their media department. Any kid with experience can serve there."

So much for hoping she'd understand. You'd think after all these years, I'd accept Mom wasn't wired for diplomacy.

"He felt disrespected. Would you apologize? I know you weren't minimizing his church, but it'd be good to clear the air since he's family."

"I said nothing wrong." Mom crossed her arms.

"You insulted his church." I extended my hand.

"He acts as though his is the only one God is moving through."

"You're deflecting. Call and apologize."

"Fine, but don't let him recruit you."

I sat on the barstool at the island counter. "Don't worry. He expects me to work as a freelancer. Vegas is *not* in the picture. Pres is committed to our church here."

She exhaled. "Thank God."

"Pres and I are having a Tulsa reception."

She smiled, probably planning the event in her mind. "It's the least she could do, considering you both live here."

"And she's staying out of planning that event, so I could use your help to throw a great reception. Something *simple* and outdoors with family and close friends."

"The Philbrook Gardens is perfect if you wait until later in the fall. A five-piece orchestra will provide a serene mood, and we can eat a five-course meal in a tent. I'll call Lauren, and we can start planning." She grabbed another mug, filled it with wassail, and took a long sip.

The more she talked, the more I envisioned something simpler: sitting at picnic tables in the woods, eating barbecue, playing cornhole. Edison lights strung above our heads from tree to tree.

Dad came inside, carrying a silver tray covered with a foil tent. "Hey, son."

"Hey." I grabbed the tray and set it on the kitchen counter. I lifted the foil to release the sweet aroma of charcoaled meat with pink juices oozing out. No one could grill like Dad. "I'm ready to dig in."

Mom grabbed formal Christmas plates lined in gold. I'd rather eat with paper plates, but they didn't belong on her elegant dining room table.

Dad sat at the head, Mom to his right, and I on his left across from her. I stayed quiet, brainstorming a way to sell my woodlands theme. But as Dad prayed, I pictured Pres swatting flies away from her face and Mom complaining that the food truck line was too long. Yet, if I didn't assert what I wanted now, I might as well kiss my vision for a casual reception goodbye. We could have the area sprayed and book multiple food vendors.

"Everything okay, son?" Dad asked after he said *amen*.

"Yeah, just a lot going on."

"Although Garrett and Pres are having the wedding in Vegas—" Mom's tone was sharp, "—they're having a Tulsa reception. So, I'll call the Philbrook and see what dates are available."

Dad looked at me. "We'll cover the expenses for the reception."

"Thanks." I shifted in my seat. "I think something more casual than the Philbrook would be good. It'll not only save a lot of money but time—"

"Don't worry about the money or the time," Mom said. "I'll throw myself into planning, and if necessary, we can hire an event planner. And the Philbrook is so elegantly situated, we won't need too many florals or décor."

"What he needs, love, is support for what they want." Dad reached for Mom's hand, but she didn't take it.

"You weren't here, but Garrett's recruiting us to help him plan the reception since Vegas will align with Pres's vision more than his."

"It's important *he* has the elements he wants," Dad said.

I set my fork down, hoping he'd win, yet discomforted as memories of their bickering replayed in my mind.

"The Philbrook has elements of nature and can be casual." Uh-oh... Mom's edginess, especially since she stared at her plate, meant she wasn't ready to buy into my vision. But she knew better than to push me, for now.

"I'm sure if you want food trucks, they'd accommodate." Dad looked at Mom.

I nodded, thankful I had an ally.

She winced. "A reception still needs to be formal. Food and entertainment are everything."

I didn't want to fight over this anymore, not after the back and forth I already endured with Pres. I cared more about being married. "The Philbrook it is but keep it low-key and intimate. Meaning..." I paused to show Mom this wasn't up for debate. Her eyes grew big, reading my resolve. "No more than seventy-five people."

She frowned. "We have our work cut out for us. Maybe relax the dress code to semi-casual with sundresses, ties, and long pants? And retain a stringed musical quintet."

"That's headed in a better direction." I winked.

"Good. Now, just so I understand, if Pres is giving us free rein with the reception, do you have a voice with the Vegas wedding?"

"It's *our* wedding. So, that reminds me. I want to include Granny and Gramps. I'd like to have their wedding picture on the memory table."

Times like these, I wished Gramps and Granny Mason could witness my wedding. They played an important role in my life; it didn't seem right that only their picture would represent their "presence." At least, my paternal grandparents would be there.

"Thank you." Mom touched her chest. "We can go through the pictures, but I have a few framed."

"Great. Also, I'd like Pres to wear Granny's bracelet as her something borrowed."

"She might not want to wear it, depending on her gown. She isn't the vintage type."

I gritted my teeth. How many times did she assume she knew people better than I did? I needed a win, so I wasn't going to back down. "We'll see."

Mom tossed the napkin on the table. "I know I'm right."

"You realize this is about honoring Granny?"

"Of course, but I'm preparing you for her reaction." Mom tapped her wrist. "She won't like the bracelet. It's too colorful."

"It's his bracelet, honey," Dad said with a flat tone.

"But it's in my keeping."

"Elena." He extended his hand toward her.

She scowled and folded her hands in her lap. "Ask Presleigh what she expects us mothers to wear. Hopefully, not some god-awful fuchsia or lavender. They don't flatter my skin."

I paused. "We're having a black-tie affair."

"Good. I'm sure she'll want us to wear gold or silver."

"Sorry... um... She wants all guests, including family and groomsmen, to wear black."

Her eyes grew large.

"Are you okay?" I asked.

"Is this a joke?" Her glare could've drilled a hole in my head.

I wanted to say, "I'm afraid not," but she'd capitalize on my reluctance and push me to change Pres's mind. So, I answered, "No."

"Like a funeral?" She set her palms on the table with a thud.

"More like an elegant soiree. It'll look sharp in pictures."

"Honey," Dad said. "Let Garrett and Presleigh work out their own wedding."

"I'm making sure his voice is heard. Presleigh is a type-A personality. If he doesn't speak up, she'll have it all planned without his input."

"Seriously?" I said.

"She's not the only one, is she?" Dad interjected.

"I've needed to be, since I'm surrounded by the most laid-back men God created." Mom attacked the creamed spinach with her fork.

Sometimes I wondered how my parents found each other. Mom overflowed with savoir faire but had a flash-in-the-pan-temper. Dad was a nature lover with a melancholy bent. The more Mom pushed, the more he retreated to his garden. That combination was a spark igniting a wildfire. I was caught in between, seeking refuge in my room, my photography, and alcohol. During my addiction recovery, they sought marital counseling and found a way to fight fair.

Once we finished dinner, Dad told Mom to relax while we cleared the table and cleaned the kitchen. She returned to making bows. Dad and I raided her homemade peppermint bark. We stood near the kitchen counter with the Christmas tin opened, popping pieces in our mouth. Her bark was a holiday favorite—a thin layer of semi-sweet chocolate topped with a thin layer of white chocolate and crushed candy canes. I considered it my reward for confronting Mom.

"Would you retrieve Granny's bracelet?" I whispered.

"Sure. Do you mind if I ask you a question?" Dad put the bark in the fridge.

"Shoot."

"What will the bracelet mean to her?"

"You know. We're merging families." *Great answer.*

"You're on a journey." Dad washed his hands then walked down the hall.

When he returned, he carried a purple velvet sack. Mom jumped up and met him near the island where I sat. "May I?" she asked.

He handed her the sack.

She faced me. "Ask Presleigh to keep the bracelet in the jewelry box and place the box in the cinched sack."

"Thanks." I reached for the sack, but she held onto it.

"Wash your hands first."

"You haven't heard of chocolate diamonds?"

"You're incorrigible."

After I washed my hands, I held them in front of her. "Do they pass inspection?"

"Yes." She rolled her eyes. "Don't leave it unattended in the car. Always keep it in the velvet sack until you present it to her. You know what? Why don't I drop it off Saturday morning?" She kept a tight grip on the sack, like when she struggled to drop me off at daycare that first time.

"You can't hold onto it forever," Dad said.

"Let me handle this." Mom shooed him away. He sat on the stool. I took a step back, not wanting to hear them go another round.

"It's easier to get it now," I said.

Mom handed me the sack. "I hope you understand that I want you to find someone who loves and respects you."

I remembered her sour expression the night of the proposal. "Where is this coming from?" I asked.

"I just..." She looked at Dad. I wouldn't doubt he had asked Mom to keep her opinions about Pres to herself. He shook his head to keep her in check. "I want you to be happy," Mom said.

"I've never been happier." I sat on a barstool next to Dad, giving myself distance from Mom. Did she just insinuate Pres and I wouldn't have a great marriage?

Dad patted my back. "Since you and Presleigh had a whirlwind romance, your mom and I will enjoy getting acquainted with her at Christmas."

Christmas vacation... I'd need that after all this drama. I was thankful Pres agreed to spend vacation with us. Since my cousin Caroline was getting married in Northern Michigan on the Friday before Christmas, Mom thought it'd be fun to stay up north for the holiday. My parents booked a farmhouse close to the Maxwells, my brother-in-law's parents.

Serendipitously, my cousin lived about thirty miles from Shane's parents. Call me sentimental, but I always liked the idea of having a community of extended family nearby. But most of us cousins and in-laws were hundreds of miles apart.

"You'll discover her fun, congenial, and generous side," I said. Once Mom would get acquainted with Pres, they'd get along, connecting over their tendency to be organized, scheduled, and direct.

"That's the point," Mom said. "Whirlwind. Will you have premarital counseling? Have you discussed if you want children? Does she like to go hiking and camping?" So typical, Mom assuming I was ignorant about life.

I shook my head. "I wish you'd trust me."

"You have no idea how much I trust you." Mom approached and laid a hand on my shoulder. "It's difficult to trust her when we hardly know her. Not because I haven't tried, but she doesn't seem interested in getting to know us."

"You know that it goes both ways, right? Have you invited her to your Bible studies or your spa outings? Taken her out to lunch?"

"That's not the only reason I have issues," she said. "But I hope she proves me wrong."

"I'm headed home. Thanks for dinner." I stood, too exhausted to hear more problems Mom perceived Pres had.

"I'll walk you to the door," Dad said.

"Love you." Mom hugged me.

"You too." My arms went limp.

Once Dad and I were outside, I put my vest on. The temps were dropping with a slight wind, but that was how I liked it. Tulsa could get frigid, but winter was a brief blip before we'd hit a warm spring and then a scorching, drench-your-face-with-sweat summer. I could endure hiking in the near-freezing temps, but I couldn't tolerate 110 rising to 120 degrees with the heat index.

"We want the best for you. Mom's making sure you're represented. If it causes division between you and Presleigh, I'll remind her to ease up."

"Appreciate that." I hugged him. "I'm looking forward to life after the wedding."

"I had the same view when I was in your situation. But life isn't about what's ahead, but digging into the mundane, challenging moments because that's where the good stuff hides."

"I'll keep that in mind."

After I drove away, I was miffed at how Mom planted a seed of doubt Pres might not want to wear the heirloom. But after I got home, I looked at the bracelet. The pearls and the gem clasp radiated. I'd tell Pres how the heirloom was custom made with precious stones and rare pearls. Show her the serial number on the clasp, proving its authenticity. Hopefully that would seal the deal since Pres liked the finer things in life.

Chapter 4

That first month of us dating, Pres struggled with me not having Friday and Saturday nights off. But we soon got into a rhythm, going out on Sunday nights instead.

So, with the bracelet in my possession, I needed to plan a memorable date. Fortunately, I had a Saturday brunch wedding to shoot, and I'd get off by four. So, I asked Pres if she'd want to go to Winterfest that Saturday night. She squealed loud and squeezed my neck tight; I was ten feet tall. Then taking a page out of Pres's book, I pre-bought tickets for the Winterfest activities and reserved a table at our restaurant.

Now it was Saturday evening. Before I picked her up, I double knotted the velvet sack that held the jewelry box then placed it in my camo bag.

I padded the sack with winter accessories for us. She underdressed in winter, saying she hated looking like a marshmallow, but they forecasted it to drop into the low thirties. I didn't want the cold weather to interfere with the ambiance. Everything had to go perfectly.

When I picked her up at her apartment, I took a step back as her skinny leather pants showed off her long legs. Good thing we had a short engagement.

After we kissed, I complimented her. "You looked gorgeous, baby."

"And we match! I like your grey cable-knit sweater." She touched the sweater near my heart. "Is it new?" I breathed a sigh of relief as she approved of my fashion choice, especially since it matched her grey crop sweater. *Great start, Bettencourt.*

"Yeah, Lauren chose it, saying it'd look great on me. So, are you ready?"

"Let me grab my coat and gloves."

Another check off my list—she was dressing warm enough.

Winterfest was Tulsa's contribution to offer locals trendy nostalgia at Christmas. Located downtown on a side street next to the sleek, glass Bank of Oklahoma stadium, the event featured a forty-foot live Christmas tree in the center, decorated with blinking-colored lights and a crystal star topper. They constructed a temporary outdoor ice rink behind the tree. Classical Christmas tunes played from tall speakers stationed throughout. I'd shot events here for clients, but I never made the time to experience it until now.

After we spent an hour ice-skating, I led her to the most romantic aspect of the date.

"Which carriage do you want?" I asked, pointing to the two types, a Vis-à-vis with a curved top like out of a Dicken's novel and the Cinderella carriage shaped like a pumpkin and covered in white lights.

"That one." Pres pointed to the Cinderella carriage. I expected her to choose this type, not because she fantasized about being a Disney princess, but because it glowed brightly like the Vegas strip. You'd think from listening to her, Vegas was in the Garden of Eden.

I paid for the ride at a booth then approached the carriage driver. Although adorned in conventional uniform with the towering top hat, tux, and black leather gloves, he wore brown cowboy boots with silver heels. Only in Oklahoma.

I smiled. "We're your next customers."

He tipped his hat. "Get on in."

I helped Pres inside then sat next to her on the royal blue padded seats. I spread the wool blanket they provided across her legs.

"Will you be warm enough?" I asked.

She snuggled close to me. "It's colder than I expected."

"Here." I reached into my camo bag and gave her hand warmers, a neck scarf, and a wool hat. After grabbing the jewelry box, I put it in my jacket pocket and zipped it closed. Now, I just needed to wait for the opportune moment.

"I'll take everything but the hat," she said. "It'll mess up my hair."

After I stuffed the hat in my bag, she asked me to take a selfie. That was something I could do well. As I prepped the shot, the carriage driver offered to take our picture. Before I could say no, Pres said, *of course*, then asked me to hand him my phone. He captured three shots, but all of them had this clown of a festivalgoer photobombing us from behind the carriage.

"Hey, sir," I said to the driver, wanting him to wait until I took the selfies myself. But he took off. Since Pres wanted to enjoy the ride, she didn't want any more pictures taken. Oh well. I'd have another opportunity.

Clomp, clomp, clomp. The hooves of the white Clydesdale horses hit the pavement in a smooth, lulling rhythm, and I relaxed as Pres leaned into my chest. Her perfume, the crisp air, and the holiday tunes whispered, *this is your moment.*

I grabbed the sack out of my pocket, but a car swerved, almost hitting the carriage. Instinctively to protect Pres, I shielded her with my body. The driver steered us toward the right curb, and I lost my balance. I grabbed the carriage frame with my left hand to steady myself. My right hand gripped the sack.

"Sorry, folks," the carriage driver said, looking behind at us. "That driver was texting and not keeping his eyes on the road."

She was almost kissing the seat, so I extended my hand to her. She took it and sat upright.

"We're fine." I put the sack in my pocket. It'd be better to wait until the restaurant.

The driver nodded. "It's still a beautiful night for a fine-looking couple."

When I planned this date, I didn't imagine the carriage driver jumping into our conversation. You'd never see that in a Hallmark movie.

"Thank you. It's obvious you're an experienced driver," Pres said. "I'm curious, how do you keep busy throughout the year?"

I squeezed her hand, irritated she was engaging with him, but she whispered, asking me to ease up. So, I released my grip, laying my hand on my lap.

"We get hired for weddings and funerals. When I took over from my father-in-law, I told my wife our motto could be, 'We marry 'em and bury 'em.'" His words flowed like a water hose.

She and the driver laughed like longtime friends, while I sulked in the seat. But I couldn't let the night get away, so I kissed her on the cheek.

"Are you warmer?" I hoped to divert her attention and remind the driver we were on a date. He turned back to face the horse, finally.

"I'm enjoying the ride," Pres said, more to him than to me.

Stiffening, I looked around. The high-rise buildings radiated with white, green, and red lights. Streetlamps glowed with metallic lit wreaths, Santas, and candy canes. I should have felt festive.

After the ride, I assisted Pres out of the carriage. Then she touched the carriage frame. "Tip him a ten. He was entertaining."

I grabbed my wallet from my jeans' back pocket. I only had a twenty.

"Even better," she said.

I handed the driver the money, wishing I had a five. I didn't have a decent selfie as a memory.

She smiled as we made our way towards the street. "Thanks, Gar Bear, for the carriage ride. Marry 'em and bury 'em will be the highlight of the night."

I feigned a weak smile, wanting to say, *I hope not.* But I said, "He was talkative."

"You were too quiet."

Tonight, our social dynamic clashed at the wrong time. "I didn't expect him to chime in," I said with a defensive tone.

"He was entertaining."

"More like unprofessional." I directed us to the sidewalk. "He needed to focus on driving. I caught him staring at us more than the street."

"It's not a big deal. The horse has the route memorized." She waved as if to dismiss my point of view.

An icy wind blew.

I thought of the bracelet. "Are you hungry?"

"I hate when you do that." Pres looked away as we waited at the crosswalk. People were laughing and talking; we should be as relaxed.

"Do what?" I asked. Subtext confused me.

"Get in one of your moods because you were mad at the driver." She crossed the street just a few seconds before the walking symbol lit up on the streetlamp.

"Pres," I shouted. "Wait until the light signals you to go." I scampered to catch up.

"There weren't any cars coming." She rolled her eyes. "Anyway, are you still hung up on the driver?"

I held her hand. "I wanted to be left alone with you."

"Some days, you tolerate people. Others, you're the life of the party. And days like this, you're a Debbie Downer."

"I'm sorry. It's just, I have a surprise for you, so I wanted this date to be perfect."

She lifted her chin. "Baby, being with you makes it perfect, especially on a rare Saturday date. But can you give me a hint about this gift?"

Pres was one of the most impatient people I knew. She'd read the ending of a novel only halfway through.

"You'll know at the restaurant. You'll love it. I promise." I kissed the top of her head.

Chapter 5

Once we got into my Jeep, I slipped the bracelet sack into my camo bag and drove to Elote Cafe, a locally owned restaurant. After we parked, I grabbed her hand since she turned toward the door.

"Can you wait a sec?" I asked. To avoid any distractions, I'd present it now.

"Let's do this inside." She shivered.

Although I put the hardtop on the Jeep, the short drive wasn't long enough to warm it up. Pres's nose and cheeks were still red.

"Sure." I adopted a fake smile. I might never get the chance to present this bracelet.

She opened the door and headed inside before I could emerge from the Jeep. Typical. She moved fast, not waiting for me to catch up. If I wasn't going to present the bracelet, I would've asked her to slow down. But with her irritated about my attitude, it wasn't the time to confront her.

Elote Cafe—where we had our first date—was an eclectic Mexican restaurant with bright yellow, green, orange, and blue walls. Cacti and other succulents lined the windowsill, reminding me of a cantina in Cancun. In the adjoining room, they kept a stage area for karaoke nights and wrestling, although those events weren't my thing.

A young woman led us to a table near the hostess station. I'd prefer to sit in the back, but the hostess said they were packed. Pres scooted into the booth, and I sat next to her.

Within a few minutes, a ginger-haired waiter approached. "Welcome. How are you tonight?" he asked.

"We're great," Pres said, quick on the draw.

"Good. I'm Jaime, your server. Can I start you off with anything to drink?"

"I'll have a virgin strawberry margarita," Pres said.

"Same here," I said, happy we could agree on that.

"I like your Celtic tat." Pres pointed to his bicep.

His tattoo was just below his T-shirt cuff. "So, you know about the tree of life?" He didn't have an Irish accent.

She smiled wider than she had all night. "I have a friend from Belfast."

I wasn't jealous, just concerned that she'd hit it off with him like she did with the carriage driver. But why should I be surprised? No one was a stranger to Pres. By the end of the night, she could write this guy's biography. As an introvert, I could just chill and listen if I wasn't in the mood to talk.

"Brilliant," Jaime said. "My mom's also from Belfast."

"Does she live in Ireland?" Pres asked.

"No, she moved here when my folks got married, but we visit every summer."

"Same with my friend. He lives here, but his family lives in Belfast."

What? I tugged on my sweater's collar. The room became smothering hot. Was she referring to her ex, Ciaran? She told me that he resided in Ireland.

"God's country," Jaime said, then he looked at me. "Would you like to start with an appetizer?"

"Pres?" I asked.

"Just house chips and salsa," she said.

"That's all," I said to Jaime.

When he left, I turned to Pres. "Ciaran?"

"What?" She muffled her voice.

"Your ex." My pulse raced. I was reliving the scene when I confronted Morgan about cheating on me. I never thought I'd have to worry about Pres.

"Yes." She looked at the menu.

"I didn't know he moved back here. When did this happen?"

"Dad hired him as the youth pastor in May. I didn't mention that?" She continued looking at the menu, instead of at me.

36

A strange sensation ran down my leg—a knowing that I should've been more alert.

"No. I would've remembered." That meant her ex moved back a month after Pres and I started dating. I straightened in my seat, irritated she didn't give me a heads-up, especially when we visited Vegas over the summer. Was she worried I'd act jealous and embarrass her when we visited? Or was she afraid I'd pick up on signs that she still cared for him?

Her hazel eyes connected with mine. Something was up because they shifted from coral green to greenish grey, like algae.

"When were you going to tell me?" I asked, trying hard to not sound paranoid.

"It's irrelevant." She waved her hand to dismiss me. "I've moved on. And we promised we wouldn't dwell on our exes."

"Are you convincing yourself or me?" I gripped the camo bag, wondering if I should go to Vegas. Yet I couldn't do that to my clients or my business.

"Don't be jealous. He's a *friend*." Pres glared, warning me to back off.

"When we were in Vegas this summer, was he there?" I continued my interrogation.

"No, I think he was on a camping trip. I would've introduced you otherwise." She touched her forehead. Was that to jog her memory? Or overdramatizing, denying her attraction for this dude?

"I need to use the restroom." Pres tapped my arm.

While she was gone, I needed to regather my confidence. Just before I met Pres, I had vowed I'd never get blindsided by a cheating partner again.

"Why are you rushing this decision?" a man's voice behind me said. Where had I heard him before? Like my dad, he talked in a dignified tone. I'd tag him in his fifties or early sixties. I turned and saw his face, but I couldn't make him out. A woman sat across from him, so I only caught the back of her head. I turned back quickly, hoping they didn't notice me staring.

"The condo is a brilliant investment," the woman responded in a tense tone with a quicker release. I didn't recognize her voice but assumed she was younger than the man. "Only Jordan could negotiate such a deal. He's buying it close to cost."

"How much is a unit selling for?" the man asked. "Not at his cost, but the listing price?"

"Five fifty."

"And how much is he purchasing it for?"

"Three hundred. See? It's too lucrative to pass up." Her tone was high-pitched, probably to convince herself.

"So, how much would you invest?"

"Half of the down payment, so thirty."

"Are you renting it out?"

I'd become absorbed into their conversation as if watching reality TV. Hey, I preferred hearing others' drama than experiencing my own.

"Hear me out," the woman said. "We're, well... I know you don't approve, but we'd live there."

Why did my heart sink? With my drinking issues and family problems, I struggled with commitment. But five years into my sobriety, I desired to have stronger relationships. Now that I was thirty and Pres was twenty-five, our engagement reinforced our maturity and trust. I couldn't imagine taking the risk of cohabitating while splitting the mortgage.

"Celine, I have red flags about this joint tenancy, much less the idea of you two moving in together. You're getting more entangled without a spiritual and legal commitment. What if your relationship doesn't work out? Once you sign the agreement, you're obligated to pay for that investment regardless of whether you're together or not." He paused. "How about this? What if you buy a condo on your own, and we pay your down payment?"

"Are you bribing me because you don't want Jordan and me to live together? Seriously?" Her voice rose five decibels; I expected her to leave the restaurant.

"Babe?" Pres placed her hand on my shoulder. I twitched as she caught me off guard. "I need to get in."

"Sorry." I scooted out of the booth.

Once we were settled, I glanced at my jacket. *Should I show her the bracelet now? Or wait until I drop her off at her apartment?* While I debated, Jaime approached, placing our drinks, a basket of chips, and small containers of homemade salsa on the table. Pres engaged in conversation with him, something about Ireland.

Yeah, I better present it now. And if she took it wedding gown shopping, it'd remind her that she was marrying *me*. Gah! Morgan's shadow still haunted me. I grabbed my bag and poked around for the velvet sack.

"Are you ready to order?" Jaime asked.

"I'll get the citrus salmon with the side of sweet potatoes and sauteed vegetables." Pres handed him the menu.

"Could you wait a sec?" I asked.

"Take your time," he said.

"Have you ever visited Vegas?" Pres asked him.

"A few times. It's a happening place."

"It's where I'm from," she said with excitement.

Not wanting to think about Pres visiting Vegas soon, I tuned them out and focused on what I wanted to eat. To make it easy on myself, I chose something familiar. "I'll have the El Nino beef burrito and chicken tortilla soup." I handed him the menu.

"Good choices," Jaime said. "I'll be back with your orders soon."

Once he left, I didn't want to waste time. I showed her the sack. "This is for you to wear at the wedding. It's your 'something borrowed'."

She tilted her head. "We never discussed my something borrowed, have we?"

"This is the surprise." I set the velvet sack in her palm.

After she opened the jewelry box, her eyes drooped, and a frown formed. This wasn't the expression I expected. "Is this the bracelet your Granny wore in that picture?"

"Yes." I lifted it out of the box, opened the gold lobster clasp, and wrapped it around her left wrist. Her hand jerked.

"It's cold," Pres said.

"I'm sorry, but I wanted to present it before our food came."

"It's beautiful but too colorful for the wedding." Pres touched the pearls.

I cringed, recalling Mom's words that Pres wouldn't like it. "Only the clasp," I said. "I'll tell you what. Why don't you take it with you when you go dress shopping next week? Make sure it goes with your gown."

"I'm not selecting my gown around the bracelet." She flipped her hair back.

Lord, give me patience; otherwise, I might demand she wear it.

"Pearls look good with any gown," I said. "And I envisioned you walking down the aisle wearing the bracelet."

"Could the photographer Photoshop the gems out?"

Her flippant attitude slapped the sentiment out of me. If it wasn't for the vision of the woman in red and wanting to prove Mom wrong, I would've backed down. "No!"

Pres's eyes grew large, taken aback by my force. I took a deep breath. She needed to understand its significance. "Each gem represents different values—"

"Let's talk about this later. Your Granny meant so much to you." She gave me a brief kiss then took a sip of her drink. The gems reflected a rainbow of colors through the glass.

"Let's put the bracelet in the box," I said.

"It's not costume jewelry?"

I jerked my head. "No, it's Akoya pearls from Japan with mined gemstones. It's probably worth at least—" I whispered in her ear, "—ten thousand dollars."

I relaxed. She just didn't realize its value.

She gasped. "Seriously?"

"Which is why it's best to protect it."

After she removed the bracelet, I put it in the jewelry box, protected that in the sack, and placed it in my camo bag.

"I'll bring it when I take you to the airport," I said.

"That works. Speaking of Vegas..." She tapped the table with her fingernails. "My mom texted me some houses for sale in her neighborhood. What if..." She took a sip of her drink, looking away.

"Where are you headed?" I asked, concerned.

"Would you mind if I checked some while I'm there?"

"Why?" I stopped eating chips. I wasn't the only one with a surprise.

"Hear me out. If we buy the house now, we won't have to juggle that after our wedding. Dad would probably help us with the down payment."

"Wait, wait, wait...slow down." I paused, wondering if I heard her right. "Did you say, we could buy a house in Vegas? Because if you did, we've never discussed leaving Tulsa."

"Look, babe, I'm planning for the future." Pres grabbed my hands. "We have this incredible opportunity in a prime neighborhood, but we need to act fast. The developer and the real estate agent attend Dad's church, so they'd give us a deal."

Why was I shocked that she operated in hard light? No filtering, shadows, or clouds, just full illumination.

"We're not living in Vegas," I said. I couldn't believe she had discussed with her family about us buying property without consulting me first. I couldn't have this dynamic in our marriage.

She bit her lip then scooted closer to me. "What if we could visit a few months out of the year and rent it as a vacation home for the other months? Not only would it pay for itself, but we'd make about three to four grand a month as passive income."

"It's hardly passive income with all the upkeep and managing each booking. It's not conducive for a low-maintenance lifestyle." I sipped on the virgin margarita, wishing there was tequila in it.

"My family would help manage the house until we considered living there longer."

I spewed the drink all over Pres's sweater. "What?" I couldn't endure more than a month or two there. If it weren't for family in Tulsa, I'd live in a cabin in the Rockies.

"That's gross." She stood as our server approached. "Excuse me, Jaime, but we could use some paper towels."

After he set our food on the table, he left to do Pres's bidding. I dipped my clean napkin into my untouched water and reached out to her sweater. She casually moved my napkin away, dismissing me. But she couldn't be as angry as I was.

"I've got it." She reached into her handbag, pulled out a stain remover stick, and dabbed the stain. When Jaime returned with paper towels, she took one sheet and pressed on the stain lightly. He wiped the table with the others.

I faced a similar dynamic as I had with Morgan. She wanted to reach a certain career goal before we got engaged, so I went along despite wanting to be married. I had convinced myself to go along because I supported her desires, but in hindsight, I was a coward, afraid she'd break up.

Imagine my excitement when Pres wanted to get married before reaching other milestones. It was one reason I proposed within seven months of dating. Why wait? But now, it was dawning on me how much we glossed over in our excitement to marry.

"Sorry, Pres, but until we discuss this thoroughly, I prefer you not looking at properties while you're in Vegas." I shook my head.

"You're right, I should've brought it up earlier." She scrunched her nose. "It's just that with all the hecticness since the engagement, I didn't make the time. Partially because it's a no-brainer! Vegas has more to offer a talented artist like you. And since Dad's church is thriving, I want to assist with their women's ministry. You could take photos for their website and social. Vegas could be our landing base for six to seven months of the year."

Her message was full of motion blur as I couldn't process her words fast enough. Landing base... Six... seven months. That's the effect of a slow shutter allowing too much light in. The joke was on me. I was the "camera" letting all her ideas into our relationship.

"I'm confused," I said. "You told me a few weeks ago, Believers Church is training you for the woman's pastor position. And I've worked extremely hard on building a successful photography business here. I'm booked two years out, so I wouldn't entertain living there part time until then."

"I understand." She laid her hand on top of mine. "It's more like a stepping-stone to what we're called to do. We could have a base in Vegas and in Tulsa and travel half the year—me on speaking engagements, you shooting weddings."

I looked at the camo bag, exhausted by the flip-flop of emotions. This night hadn't gone the way I expected. Was I stuck by not pursuing nature photography? And Pres was God's way of pushing me out of my comfort zone? I held my breath, wondering if that wall of defense was my enemy, keeping me from moving forward.

"It's too much to process, right now," I said.

"Let's focus on our wedding, then. Have you picked between the two choices I sent you for the first dance?"

"I thought we agreed not to do wedding planning on dates." If I didn't direct her, she'd have us decide the entire wedding playlist by the time we finished dinner. And with all the bombshell revelations, I couldn't make decisions right now.

Pres pushed the queso fresco to the side of the plate and then cut her salmon in square pieces. *Uh-oh.* She became more fastidious when upset. "Doesn't gifting the bracelet for the wedding make planning fair game?"

"Please, can't we enjoy tonight?"

She looked away. "Give Vegas a chance. They've got wildlife and hiking trails. It's centrally located between Yellowstone and Colorado. It's the same distance to Denver as Tulsa."

"We've got time to plan our future once we're married," I said as firm as I could.

"Maybe..."

For the rest of the date, we danced around subjects because I couldn't focus on much of anything. I was relieved she'd wear the bracelet but concerned about where we'd end up. Pres was a force; she'd continue pressing until I caved in. When I kissed her at her apartment door, her body felt stiff like a mannequin. Oh well. Like Mom, she'd rebound to a happier attitude by tomorrow.

Chapter 6

On most Mondays, after a hectic weekend of shooting weddings and often Sunday post-celebration brunches, I didn't get out of bed until after nine in the morning. I'd lounge in my joggers and a tee, tinker in the backyard, photograph birds, and go hiking or to the climb gym.

By two, I'd meet up with Pres. She liked to knock off eight items on her to-do list before connecting with me.

But on this particular Monday, I worked all morning, catching up before Christmas break. By four, though, I wasn't going out on a date with my girl. Instead, I was dropping her and Moriah off at the airport.

All morning, while I worked on editing Saturday's wedding, premonition and dread distracted me. Would this Vegas trip become a scouting mission for our future?

After I pulled into the departure drop-off, I turned toward Pres. "Here's the bracelet. Keep it in your purse."

She took it. "My purse is full. I'll put it in my tote."

"Okay." I leaned over and gave her a kiss.

She opened the door and slid out gracefully.

"Bye, Moriah. Monitor my girl."

"Of course." Moriah grabbed her backpack.

An empty grocery bag lay near the backpack. I got out of the Jeep, grabbed the bag, then approached Pres as she reached into the back seat to retrieve her navy tote.

"Hey," I said. "Put the sack with the bracelet inside this bag. That way, no one will see the box except airline security. Or you could even wrap your underwear around the box. Then no one will suspect there's a priceless piece of jewelry inside."

"I will once I get checked in."

I walked to the back of the Jeep, grabbed her larger navy suitcase, and placed it near her feet.

She smiled. "I'll call when we arrive in Vegas."

"You still have an hour and a half before your flight takes off, so I'll wait with you before you go through security," I said.

She hesitated, but Moriah touched her arm. "I'll go to our gate and give you updates on the flight."

"Thanks." Pres looked at me. "I'll meet you near the security line."

After I parked, I rushed inside. When I reached the TSA's security line, Pres wasn't there. I walked to the hallway, leaned on a ledge, and peered down at the first-floor check-in counter, but didn't see her. Then she emerged from the escalator, and with her head held high, she strolled down the hallway in her long boots like a model on a catwalk.

Once she reached me, she frowned. "My bag was overweight, so I had to pay extra. I'm going to get a caramel macchiato."

"I'll get it for you." I kissed her on the cheek.

"Thanks. A venti with coconut milk. No whipped cream."

"Coming right up."

Within ten minutes, I returned with her order. She talked on the phone as she sat at a table across from the restrooms. "I'll be there Wednesday night, then." Pres sounded lighthearted.

When I sat beside her, she looked at me.

"I've got to go. See you soon." She hung up the phone.

"Hey, babe, here's your latte." I set it in front of her.

"You're a lifesaver." She flashed a wide grin, then took a sip. "Hits the spot. Thanks, love."

I looked for the navy tote but didn't see it on the table, on the two empty chairs, or underneath her feet.

"Where is your bag?" I asked as my heart raced.

She looked underneath the table. "I swear it was here."

"Did you have it after you got out of my Jeep?"

"Yes. I had it in the restroom... Hold on." She stood, then dashed into the women's restroom.

I called Moriah hoping she'd know its whereabouts, but she didn't answer.

Pres emerged without the tote. I stood, but she rushed past, heading to the escalators. This couldn't be happening.

I followed her as she ran down the escalator, weaving past people standing stationary. I walked down, excusing myself as I tried to avoid rubbing against them. A few of them *humphed*, some asked what was wrong, but I didn't answer since my chest was too tight. I caught up with Pres near the check-in counters. She flagged a security guard standing near the airport entrance.

"Sir... I can't find my navy tote.... I had it... in the bathroom but... it was gone... when I checked for it." She wiped the sweat from her brow.

"Which restroom, ma'am?" he asked. His name badge read *Marcus*. He looked all business—a black man with muscular biceps that could crush peanuts in one squeeze.

"Upstairs near security." Pres pointed up.

"Let's head there now," Marcus said.

We rushed to the women's restroom, but I waited by the door. I was tempted to follow Marcus and Pres, but knew I'd better wait in case there were women inside. I wrung my hands as I stepped closer to the restroom.

My heart beat louder and louder, as I struggled to get my breath. But I managed a short prayer.

"Excuse me, but I need to use the restroom," a woman said.

"Sorry." I moved to the side, and within ten seconds, Pres and Marcus emerged.

"It's here," she said, smiling as she held up the carry-on.

I stopped wringing my hands. My palms were raw and red.

"You're fortunate to find it," Marcus said to Pres. "Safe travels to you both." Then he left.

I led Pres to the same table. "Where was the tote?" I asked. Did she overlook it in the stall earlier? And why didn't she notice it after returning to search that first time? Had she left it under the sink and in her panic overlooked it? Did Marcus find it?

"It was under the sink." She stuck out her lower lip. "I'm sorry for leaving it in there. I got distracted trying to plan everything I'm doing in Vegas."

Hmm... Was she talking to Ciaran? Maybe that's why she left the bag in the restroom? I couldn't afford to think like that. She was marrying me. "So, you didn't see it when you returned that first time after I noticed it was missing?"

"Yeah, although I looked under the sink, in the stall, even in the garbage—which was so gross. I mean, I didn't put my hand in there, but jiggled the can." She scrunched her face, recalling the foul odor.

"Maybe you should check if the bracelet is in there?"

"Why? It's obvious I either overlooked it, or someone mistakenly grabbed it thinking it was theirs, and then returned it to where they found it." She shrugged as her phone rang. She glanced at it. "Do you mind if I take this? It's Mom."

I nodded, despite not wanting her to take the call. I'd prefer she inspect the tote and then visit with me. But she seemed eager to answer. Their call didn't last long as Pres confirmed the plans for the week including the bridal appointment in the morning. Yada, yada. I didn't pay too much attention until Pres said something about wanting to attend youth group on Wednesday night.

Once she was off the phone, she smiled. "Sorry, Mom needed to check the flight again, and then went over the itinerary." She looked at her watch. "It's time."

I grabbed her carry-on in my left hand while holding her fingers in my right as we walked to the TSA PreCheck line. Once we reached the black ropes, I gave her a kiss.

"Keep me posted on your flight and when you land in Vegas," I said, still holding her hand.

"I will. I'm sorry I'm leaving for a week just after our engagement." She made a sour face. "But I'll call you every day."

"Don't sweat it. I just wish I could go with you." I squeezed her hand. "I love you and stay safe."

"Love you, Gar Bear." She kissed my cheek, then approached the line.

I headed to short-term parking. I hoped work would keep me distracted, so I wouldn't miss her as much. On cue, a client called as I slid into my Jeep. We chatted for about twenty minutes. Then as I drove toward the airport exit, Pres called.

"Don't freak out, but the bracelet's gone. I'm so sorry!"

I slammed on the brakes, and a driver in the truck behind me honked. I looked back, rolled down my window, and waved for him to pass. As he drove around me, he flipped me the bird.

"What's your problem?" I yelled, but doubted he heard me.

After I parked, I sprinted into the airport. Inside, Pres's voice came through my phone. "Garrett!"

"Sorry, I assumed you hung up. Let me think. Are you sure it's not in the tote? You left it in the restroom for less than five minutes."

"Moriah and I have checked the carry-on multiple times. I've emptied everything out. It's not in there. Someone... I can't believe I'm saying this, but someone must've stolen it."

It was difficult to hear her as the gate clerk announced a flight, passengers scuffled past, and conversations echoed. "Wait? Did you stay stolen?"

"Oh, this is bad... I can't believe it. I'm so sorry!"

Yes, I heard her right, but instead of panicking, I went into command mode. "Have you notified security? TSA?"

"Immediately before calling you."

"Lost and Found?"

"I'll check. I'll call you back."

After I hung up, I prayed out loud. "God, we need one of those 'coin in the fish's mouth' miracles. Let it show up in Lost and Found. Please."

Pres called shortly. "Babe, you'll have to check Lost and Found. It's on your side of the airport."

"I'm headed there now. Keep me updated?" I said.

Marcus walked by. Hey, a sign. I stopped him, and he informed me they were searching for the bracelet. Then before I could ask, he directed me to Lost and Found.

Fortunately, it was around the corner. When I reached the office, I hung my head. Why was everything against me? They were closed for the day. The lights were off, the door locked. I took a picture of the office hours painted on the door, then made a calendar notification on my phone. Call L & F at 7 a.m.

I sat in a nearby chair and ran through several scenarios. If anyone found it, would they let Pres know first? What if she was in the air?

I called her. "Babe, can you catch a later flight? If they recover the bracelet, it'd be good if you're still at the airport."

"Okay..." She sounded distant. "I'll check and let you know."

Within ten minutes, she called. "I'm sorry, but all the flights are full. I'll have to fly out on this one."

"Can't you catch one tomorrow and reschedule your bridal appointment?" I asked.

"Airport security is checking everyone's carry-ons. And the boutique owner arranged for a babysitter tomorrow. I can't cancel."

I wanted to say, the owner's inconvenience was minor compared to this disaster, but I knew it wouldn't change her mind. So, in anger, I said, "I should've just given you the bracelet at the wedding."

"Forgive me. This is horrible."

"Why didn't you put it in your purse? I knew you should've wrapped the jewelry box in a Walmart bag or your underwear. Something inconspicuous."

"But I didn't." Her voice was sharp.

"I should've held your tote when you used the restroom."

"Stop treating me like a child."

"You do not know what that bracelet means to my family. They won't forgive me for losing it." I raised my voice, not meaning to, but couldn't help it as I got angrier by the second.

"No, they won't forgive *me*... Look, they're announcing our flight. I'll call when I'm in Vegas. I love you."

"Love you," I mumbled.

Pres groaned before she hung up, but I couldn't pretend to be saccharine. If we didn't recover it, I'd lose Granny *again*.

I found the phone numbers for TSA, Tulsa's airport security, and for each airline. I stayed at the airport for two more hours, so I bought a large frozen mocha and a blueberry muffin. Needing energy, I inhaled the mocha long before I finished the muffin. It was difficult to eat when my mind scrutinized every theory coming through it like a turnstile.

What if the thief was flying to another state or another country? What if she sold it on the black market, so it was untraceable?

What if she kept it for herself? I wanted to hang around until all the flights departed, but Marcus assured they'd notify me if they retrieved it. How could I face Mom?

Chapter 7

I drove to the nearest police station and filed a stolen property report. This process reminded me of college orientation. I got lost on campus several times, and when school started, I arrived late to nearly all my classes that first day.

When the police officer asked me for the bracelet's serial number, a receipt, or insurance claim information, I grew silent. I didn't think to get proof of ownership from Mom earlier since I didn't need it.

I deliberated the best course of action. I didn't want to get interrogated if I called Mom, yet I didn't want to put Dad in a tight spot since I'd ask him to not tell her. The officer repeated her statement as though I hadn't understood or heard her the first time.

I went to the Jeep and called Dad. To my relief, he provided the details and assured he wouldn't let Mom know why I needed the info. I promised him I'd explain later.

Once I filed the stolen property report, I pressed the officer to visit the nearest pawnshop ASAP, so we could catch the thief red-handed. I felt like I was a victim on a crime show, reporting about a missing person and expecting the cop to drop other cases and commit their time to mine.

She informed me a detective would most likely get assigned to the case. They'd work with airport security and view the surveillance cameras. And they'd record the item in the Stolen Articles File at the FBI's National Crime Info Center and with LeadsOnline—a privately operated, national database pawnbrokers used to register items they purchased.

I was skeptical whether pawn owners would report costly jewelry, but she emphasized they were required by law; otherwise, if they got caught, they'd get shut down.

"You have ten days before the pawnshop can sell the item to a customer," the officer said.

"So, I need to visit them within a ten-day window?" If my anxiety was a ten before, it lowered to a five now. Great! I'd have the bracelet returned to me before anyone knew better.

"A detective will visit the pawnshops."

Perhaps I was paranoid, but I swear she looked me up and down and concluded I was too green behind the ears.

"I don't know when they'd go, and I'm unwilling to let a day pass by without doing something myself." I narrowed my eyes, hoping she'd understand my urgency.

"Some words of advice. I wouldn't let on you're looking for it. Instead, pretend to be a customer. Otherwise, the broker might suspect you're a thief who's reclaiming something you originally stole. They prefer to work with us, not the original owner—"

"Even if I have proof of ownership?" I asked. Welcome to the world of pawnshops.

"How does the broker know you didn't lift that info, too?"

"True." I wasn't prepared to face the complications that criminal activity poses.

"I recommend you see if he'll sell it to you. If the broker does, put on your best Oscar performance but don't buy the item. Leave and then call us ASAP or come by the station. We'll handle it. Got that?" She repeated the last statement about not confronting the pawnbroker but contacting the police instead.

"What if they don't register it but sell it under the table? Can I demand they hand it over, especially since the serial number is on the bracelet?"

"I just told you what to do in all scenarios." She shuffled papers. Surely, she wasn't moving on to a different report.

I set my hands on the counter. "Look, if I catch the bracelet at their shop, I can't walk away knowing they were evading the law. They could sell it to someone before you confront them."

She glanced at me. "Are you ready to deal with a shady pawnbroker?"

I flashed a smile, hoping to incite my courage. "Ma'am, I wouldn't be, but I'm desperate."

"Just follow the procedures I gave you."

"Alrighty," I said.

The next morning, I visited Okie Pawn, the one closest to the airport as soon as it opened. The parking lot was nearly empty. Graffiti decorated the sides of the worn building except on the pawnshop. Their storefront and one exposed side were pristinely painted white with black trim along the roofline. Metal security bars covered the windows. This wasn't a dark alley, but not where I wanted to hang out.

The bell chimed as I entered. The thick glass doors, probably bulletproof, slammed behind me, as if I'd entered a prison cell. I briefly glanced at the door, wondering if I'd made a mistake.

Do it for the bracelet, man. So, I faced the front.

The shop was square with glass displays of jewelry forming a "U" in the center. Flat screen TVs lined up along the right wall, and electronics, instruments, and cameras were lined up on the left wall. A long counter ran from wall to wall at the front of the shop. Guns were mounted behind the counter.

I approached the middle-aged pawnbroker standing behind the front register. I did a double take, since I didn't expect a guy who looked more Jersey than Okie. He wore a white shirt with brown pinstripes, beige vest, and black slicked-back hair, a real-life Michael Corleone. This was intimidating.

When his phone rang, he didn't nod or look at me, but answered the call. I waited about ten feet away, glancing at the displays to my left.

Bright orange and yellow stickers with **25%**, **35%**, and **45%** printed in black ink clung to each item. A Canon F1 camera body, no lens or straps, caught my attention. One of my childhood idols who shot for *National Geographic* gifted his F1 to me when I was a kid. I kept the camera body in the back of my closet and once I got serious about wildlife photography, I'd place it on my desk.

As the broker talked about this deal, I eavesdropped while walking toward the jewelry in the glass displays. "Jordan, tell me you're biting on this once-in-a-lifetime deal... Exactly! That's my nephew. How about I drop it off at noon? Nah, I can't wait until the weekend; it's got to be today. Good, good. See you then." He even had that thick Jersey accent.

I looked up.

"How can I help you?" he asked, placing something—which looked like a purple velvet sack—into a drawer. My heart raced.

"Ummm..." I cleared my throat and approached the counter.

"Looking for jewelry for your girl? Gold cufflinks for your boss? Tell you what—I'll cut you a deal. I've got everything at rock-bottom prices." He pulled up his sleeve, flashing a Rolex.

Should I ask to see what was in the purple sack? If he was going to sell it under the table, I could pretend I'm looking for something resembling the bracelet and buy it.

"Hello? Are you there?" He waved his hand in front of me, bringing me out of my internal debate.

"Sorry. I'm here to find a vintage pearl bracelet for my grandma. She wants one with gemstones on the clasp. She knew about this jeweler to the stars, Seaman Schepps, and remembered a distinct bracelet he custom-made for a client. Although her memory's fading—she's turning a hundred..." I paused, hoping he was sentimental. "I thought if I could find something similar like she saw in his Manhattan shop, I'd like to gift it to her. It doesn't have to be from him, just something resembling his craftsmanship. She'd think it was from him."

"Of course." He pinched his fingers in agreement. "Got to like a boy who treats his elders right."

I tapped the glass counter to show him I was ready to make a deal. "So, do you have anything like what I described? I'll drop one grand today."

He walked to the jewelry displays. "I have Art Deco pieces, so I'm sure there's something your dear grandma would like."

Although he'd be skirting the law, I hoped he had already put the bracelet out to sell. I approached the jewelry counter.

"This one is similar with two pearl strands and a gold clasp." He held a long cream box with the jewel lifted toward my face.

I shook my head. "She said it had four strands and a multi-jeweled clasp."

The man looked away for a brief second then stared at me. "Sorry, kid. I have nothing fitting that description but check back another time. I often have items that resemble the jeweler's craftsmanship. You know, from punk adult kids—of course, nothing like you—who come in here after grandma dies and pawn all her valuables. Tsk...tsk. Tragic, if you ask me."

I smiled to disguise my irritation as he seemed to insinuate I was some addict or lowlife. Why was he trying that hard to intimidate me?

"Good luck." He marched to the register.

I followed and stood across from him. "If something like that comes in, call me." I handed him my business card. "Doesn't matter the time. I'll answer." He didn't look at the card but placed it into his breast pocket of his shirt. "Can I have yours?" I asked.

"Why not?" He grabbed a card from a gold holder near the register. After he handed it to me, he shook my hand as if to warn me.

I couldn't resist going rogue, no matter what the cop advised. "By the way, I noticed you had a purple velvet sack. It resembles my grandma's. Could I look at it? Even if I can't get her the bracelet, at least I could buy that and put something similar in it." My confidence grew the more I improvised.

He pursed his lips as he glared.

"Name your price," I said.

He flicked his hand from his chin toward me. "Don't know what you saw, but if it's not out on display, it's not for sale. Capisce?"

This man had the bracelet. I shot him a toothy grin. "Come on. It's just a sack. It'd mean so much to my grandma." I grabbed my wallet. "Name your price."

"I'm afraid you didn't hear me. Look, your grandma must be a gem, and you obviously haven't stepped inside a pawnshop, but that sack belongs to a customer." He leaned toward me.

"It's collateral for a loan. And I treat every customer of mine, especially regulars, as royalty."

I was done with niceties. "Look, man. I know what's in that sack, and you know that I know. Someone sold it to you last night, didn't they? Just before you closed—"

"I know what?" He positioned his hands in a pistol position, index fingers touching his lips. I wanted to jump over the counter and grab the sack, but he had guns in a glass display by his thigh.

"I'm not a fool," I said. "If you want to stay in business, you better show it to me. I have the serial number and original sales receipt to prove it."

He banged his hand on the counter. "Settle down, Rookie. You waltz into my shop, lie about gifting an item to your grandma, but now tell me it belongs to you?" He growled like a guard dog. "I don't have it."

"Because you're selling it to your nephew under the table?" I got so close, I could see his nose flailing.

He didn't answer, so I continued. "I'm right, aren't I?"

"Don't come into my shop and try to shake me down." He wagged his finger in my face.

I didn't want to find out what he'd do if I pushed further. But I wouldn't leave without giving him something to think about. "This isn't the last time you'll hear from me. And by the way, the police will be interested in our conversation. If I find that bracelet in your nephew's possession or displayed here in ten days, I'll claim what is mine!"

He shrugged, angering me.

I drove to the police station and talked to the detective assigned to my case. After he interviewed me about the airport fiasco and my experience at Okie Pawn, he informed me that Sonny, the owner, was reputable. "A few months ago, he recorded an item flagged as stolen in the database," the detective said.

Now, I was worried the detective and Sonny were in cahoots and would split the prize money. If that was the case, I could kiss the bracelet goodbye. On cue, he assured me that he'd file an expedited search warrant. "It might take an hour or two if the judge signs off on it," he told me.

I shrugged, not getting my hopes up. I wouldn't put it past the pawn owner to move the heirloom after I had left his shop.

I visited four more pawnshops, called ten, and returned home empty-handed. Fifteen down, twenty more to go. I sat in my living room trying to regroup while I waited to hear from the detective. While I hoped they'd find the bracelet, I was skeptical.

"What have I done?" I yelled.

I laid my head on the sectional trying to calm down. I turned to face the picture of Granny on my wall. Shame, a moth, ate a hole in me.

I sprang off the couch, removed the picture off the wall, and hid it in my guest bedroom closet. "Sorry, Granny." I rushed out of the bedroom.

Pres called as I was making a grilled cheese and ham sandwich. "Baby," she said. "We're off to the bridal appointment, but I wanted to check on you. I called a pawnshop—oh, what's the name? It's closest to the airport. Anyway, the owner hasn't seen it but got snippy as if I was harassing him. I don't know what that's about."

I hung my head. "It was probably the same one I visited this morning. Guy has a hoarse voice and accent that's straight out of Jersey?"

"That's him. What time were you at the shop?" She asked.

"Nine here."

"I called about five minutes later. That explains why he was obnoxiously rude."

I almost dropped the phone. He probably moved that bracelet after Pres called. So much for the search warrant.

"But hold on to hope," Pres continued. "We'll get it back. This morning, we all prayed for the bracelet to show up."

"Thank you, baby. I hardly slept last night, afraid we'll never see it again." At least she cared about the bracelet and more importantly, about us.

"Who else have you called?" she asked in her 'let's get to business' tone. Normally, I would get a little turned off by her assertiveness when she pushed something I didn't want, but today, it worked in my favor.

"The airport's Lost and Found, but they haven't received it either. And I have twenty more pawnshops to call," I said.

"Why don't you email me a list of shops, and I'll help?" she suggested.

"Great! I'm emailing you the spreadsheet now." I grabbed my phone and sent her the doc. "Why don't you call the pawnshops on the outer edges of town, like Glenpool, Owasso, and Catoosa?"

"A spreadsheet, I'm impressed. I'll call in-between visiting venues."

"Thanks." I lifted my chest. After I ate lunch, I worked for most of the afternoon. But by five, I got antsy about the bracelet. So, I called the detective. My heart raced when he informed me they got an expedited warrant and visited the pawnshop.

"Did you find anything?" I asked, hoping they caught the owner before he left.

"Sonny was cooperative. He gave us access to the surveillance cameras from the afternoon when the bracelet was lost until he closed the shop."

"Could you see what merchandise was purchased?" I wiped my sweaty palms on my jeans.

"The camera is set on the wall behind the counter, giving us visibility to all the transactions."

"Did anyone appear desperate to sell their goods? Paranoid? Did you see if he left the shop during the day? And do the cameras cover the parking lot?"

"Slow down." He talked like he was sitting on a rocking chair, sipping sweet tea. "I'll answer all your questions one at a time."

"Yes." I omitted "sir" since he was around my age, and I didn't want to give him any more respect than that. I was miffed he didn't shake Sonny down and wrest a confession.

"No one sold jewelry to the shop yesterday. And the windows are secured with bars, obstructing a clear view of the parking lot. And I haven't viewed the footage from today—"

"How about his office, where he keeps a safe for priceless jewelry, wads of cash, or other valuables? Is there anywhere in the store where they could be out of view of the camera?" I spoke quickly as my head spun at all the ways he could've evaded detection.

"It's all on the same hard drive. I was going to say before you interrupted, I'll cross-reference the footage from Okie Pawn with airport security records to ascertain if any individual was at the airport on the day of the theft and subsequently patronized the shop. And no, he doesn't have cameras in the office."

"So, he could've made a back door transaction? I know he had a purple sack."

"Do you have photographic evidence? Sonny showed us a purple sack, but it held a wedding ring."

I grunted. "Isn't that convenient? Did you bother to ask him about meeting his nephew at lunch that day?"

"I did." The detective was even-toned, as if used to hot-headed citizens like me. "He just returned from dropping off a batch of homemade cookies for his nephew's girlfriend for her birthday. He was supposed to drop them off Monday, but it had slipped his mind. He said his wife would tan his hide if he didn't deliver them today."

"Wow. You don't believe that line of crap, do you?" I blurted. They must've assigned me a rookie.

"Everyone is a suspect in your eyes. I don't doubt you thought the broker possessed the heirloom. So, my advice is to wait and let *us* handle the investigation."

"Or we admit the pawnbroker schooled us both." I hung up, unsure who to trust.

CHAPTER 8

Mom called shortly after I talked to the detective. I let her call go to voicemail. "Hey, just wanted to check if you're home. Since you're working long hours, I made your favorite meal. We will drop it off. Let me know when it would be a good time to stop by. Love you."

When I didn't reply, she texted about fifteen minutes later: Are you home?

I just couldn't get the courage to answer. This mishap reminded me of my college days when I had to confess about my partying.

One summer weekend, when my buddy's parents were out of town, some of us from our frat house stayed with him.

Early Sunday morning, two officers came to the house, knocking on the front door as they identified themselves. Later, I discovered the next-door neighbor had called the police, complaining about beer cans and liquor bottles sprawled all over his lawn.

Since I slept on the couch downstairs, I woke up immediately. I debated running upstairs and warning my buddy, but the police continued knocking, demanding we answer. Suffering a hangover and disorientated, I panicked, expecting the police to barge in.

I opened the door and stared at Officer Peters, a friend of my parents. Once he assessed the situation, he placed his hand on my shoulder. "Garrett, tell your parents today, or I'll pay them a visit."

I told Dad then Mom since they were separated. He was disappointed but Mom erupted, grounding me for the rest of the summer. I couldn't do anything with my buddies. According to the arrangement before the party fiasco, I spent weekends with Dad at Lauren's where he stayed temporarily and with Mom during the week.

She was insufferable for the rest of the summer. She'd call Dad, making sure I was with them and not out with my buddies getting drunk or pulled over for drunk driving.

When I returned to campus in the fall, she'd call every Friday morning, asking about my weekend plans. I'd rather relive that ordeal than tell Mom about the bracelet.

This news might tank my "Pres is the right candidate" campaign.

An hour later, my doorbell rang twice. *Crap!* It was Mom. She assumed I'd be working upstairs, so she'd ring it at least twice if not three times. I wasn't ready to confess, so I needed to explain I was in the throes of editing. *Thanks for the meal, but I've got to work.*

I rehearsed this line a few times as I sauntered to the front door. As I opened it, my heart sank. Dad was with her; they were planning to visit awhile.

I plastered on my cheesiest, I-will-hug-your-babies smile. "Come in."

Dad carried a large slow cooker while Mom held a white canvas bag with tall handles. After I closed the door, I reached for the slow cooker. "I'll take that."

"No, get Mom's tote." He tilted his head toward her.

I freed her of the tote and followed Dad into the kitchen. Mom removed her camel overcoat, grabbed Dad's from him, and then hung them in the coat closet in my front entry. Hopefully, they wouldn't stay too long. As I put the canvas tote on the counter next to the slow cooker, Mom approached.

"Thanks." I patted Dad's back. "That can stay warm while I finish culling nearly a thousand images. I'll probably eat in a few hours."

"We thought you'd be too busy to answer, so we stopped by." Mom removed the glass containers of steamed asparagus, button mushrooms, mashed potatoes, and homemade rolls. The aroma of seared meat, garlic, and butter filled my kitchen and aroused my appetite. I almost forgot about the bracelet.

"It all looks delicious." I hugged her. "What did you make?"

"Beef Wellington with a green peppercorn sauce." She lifted her chin, proud to fatten her son.

"Thanks!" I exaggerated my excitement. "But if you don't mind, I need to return to work. I'll dig into it soon." I wasn't sure if she heard me the first time.

"Go for it," Dad said, but Mom pouted.

"Let me try a piece of meat," I said. "Nothing beats the flaky crust or the tender beef." I elbowed her, hoping to jar a smile.

She gave me a half smile. "Appreciate that. Let me prepare it for you." Mom got a knife from the butcher block near the oven, and I grabbed a plate.

Dad went into the living room and sat on the sectional. I was confused, wondering why he was chilling as if to stay for a while.

As Mom put the meal on a serving platter, I was riddled with guilt. Ever since I was a teen, I always requested this meal for my birthday. With both sets of grandparents joining us, we'd gather at my parents' dining room table to celebrate *me*.

Tonight, I didn't deem myself worthy of it. I glanced at Dad as he read my latest issue of *National Geographic*. Mom stood next to me, smiling as she waited for my verdict. I took a bite of beef, wanting to focus on something happy and hoping she wouldn't notice Granny's picture missing.

I ate slowly, especially since everything came together in a compatible marriage of flavors. I forgot myself. "Wow. You hit it out of the park."

"Glad you enjoy my cooking." She touched a yellow bangle on her wrist. "Also, Uncle Earl called. Caroline wants to wear the bracelet for the wedding."

Nearly choking on the piece of meat, I coughed it up onto my plate. This couldn't be happening.

"Are you all right?" Dad asked, looking over.

Mom got me a glass of water and handed it to me. "Here, take a sip."

Of all the heirloom jewelry Granny owned, my cousin wanted the bracelet.

"If you've already showed Presleigh the bracelet, I'll get it now," Mom said. "That way, we won't forget to take it to Michigan."

I closed my eyes, wishing I could teleport back to Elote Cafe. I would've only shown Pres the bracelet and not suggested she take it to Vegas. But I couldn't go back, so I opened my eyes. "It's not here at the moment."

"Where is it?" She narrowed her eyes. "You didn't give it to Presleigh to hold onto it for the wedding, did you?"

I took a long sip of water. My pulse rose to a hundred beats per minute. "Promise you won't interrupt, but let me explain?" I asked.

"Of course." She played with her bangle, rolling it over and over with her fingers. I wished she'd stop.

I looked at Dad. His eyes were closed, mouth cracked. He was asleep. If only I could be him. "I gave it to Pres to take to Vegas when shopping for a wedding gown. Well, she put the bracelet in her carry-on, and somehow, it got... stolen." I grimaced, ready for Mom to spin like a top.

Her mouth gaped, like she wanted to scream but couldn't. Then she spluttered, scowled, and shook. Her baby blues flew wide open. I wrung my hands, knowing she was going to blow.

"Are you all right?" I asked.

Mom pointed to her throat, her face ashen-white like whole milk.

I filled a glass with ice cold water and handed it to her, hoping she'd have time to process.

After she took a long drink, she grabbed a napkin and wiped the corners of her mouth. After setting the glass on the table, she shook her head, staring at me.

"Say something," I said. Her silence was torture. I wondered what she'd do as her face turned pinker by the second. The shock was wearing off.

Standing, she placed her hand on the chair. "I'm trying not to explode. I'm so, so angry. How could you? You might as well have lost Granny's ashes." She shook her head, then walked to the front entry, around the sectional, past Dad sleeping, and circled the island in the kitchen. Another round and another, while mumbling incoherent words.

"I'm sick about it." I stood near the table, gripping my abs since my stomach waltzed with my digested food.

"What have you done?" She extended her arms.

"I know it's bad—" I might as well be chained to the public stocks.

"No. What steps have you taken to recover it? And did she lose it in the Tulsa airport? On a connecting flight? Is it in Vegas?" Her face grew to a sordid shade of pinkish red. I hadn't seen her this angry since I had to confess about the party.

I told her the story of the lost bracelet, sparing no gory details. But before I could share the results of the investigation, she dove into a rant.

"I knew you shouldn't have trusted her with the heirloom."

She paced the living room again.

I turned away, angry she implied Pres was irresponsible, and I was negligent. It was one thing to think it but another to hear it from someone else's mouth.

"Who's nothing?" Dad said, his eyes opened.

Mom pointed to me as she glared at him. "His fiancée lost the bracelet. Can you believe it?" She glanced at me. "It didn't mean anything to her."

"Just don't," I said as my head spun.

"You're blindly in love." She placed her hands on her hips. "It's like she's cast a spell on you."

"Be nice, love," Dad said.

"Just because she accidentally lost the bracelet, you're calling her a witch? I don't have words..." I stood. "I've got work to do."

Dad lowered his hand, a signal for Mom to cool it. But once her top spun, it'd be difficult to get her to slow down and impossible to make her stop.

I took my plate to the sink.

"I didn't call her a witch, but I'm trying to wrap my head around how she gets you to cater to her *every* whim." Mom stood near Dad. "It's like our opinions don't matter."

"That's the problem." I rubbed my forehead where a line of tension formed. "You resent I'm answering to another woman."

"I'm sorry you see it that way." Mom turned to Dad. "I told you she'd pit him against us."

He shook his head. "That's an unfair assessment."

"There's no use staying here," Mom said like I wasn't in the room. "We've got a hot supper at home."

"Do you hear yourself? You hardly know Pres, yet you throw accusations around because she doesn't align with your expectations." I approached Mom, standing only a few inches from her. "I doubt there's any woman who could meet your exacting standards. And if you'd meet her, trust me, it'd only be a matter of time before she messed up, and you'd indict her for being unsuitable." Now, I was the spinning top.

Mom opened her mouth but stared in silence.

"That's right, you don't give people margin for mistakes." My face grew warm. "You've expected us to be perfect kids and now flawless adults."

"Why do you want to hurt me? I've sacrificed my life for you and Lauren, and this is the gratitude I get?" Mom's lips quivered.

"Sorry, son, about the bracelet." Dad lowered his voice. "She's in shock; give her time."

Even if he'd talk to her later, it wouldn't do any good. She'd need divine intervention to get clarity, but I didn't have the patience to wait that long. Her words stung.

"Come, honey." Mom turned on her heels and went to the front door. "Let's focus on recovering the bracelet. We're going to the police."

"I already filed a report," I blurted. Although I didn't want her involved in my investigation, she wouldn't stay on the sidelines. So, I got her up to speed on the case, and I ended with how Pres had been calling pawnshops.

"She should call all of them." Mom's tone was sharp.

I glared at her. "Really?"

"How can we help?" Dad asked.

I paused, gathering my composure. "I've covered midtown, downtown, and near the airport. Why don't you check the ones south of 71st and Riverside? I'll print you a copy."

"Thank you," she said. "At least you have a strategy, but all of this would be unnecessary—"

"Honey." Dad patted her shoulder. "Garrett's doing everything he can. We need to support him."

She jerked her arm away. "Easy for you to say. It didn't belong to your mom."

Ouch! I jumped, but Dad didn't flinch as his hands fell to his side. "I loved Granny," he said.

I turned to the left, went down the hallway, and up the stairs, skipping every other step. I didn't want to hear them arguing. In my office, I closed my eyes to center myself. *Pause when you're triggered* was a tool my counselor taught me.

Once my pulse stopped racing, I opened my eyes. I got to work, printing a copy of the war plans and highlighting the shops I assigned to my parents. As I returned to the living room, Dad stood near the sectional, and Mom, with her overcoat on and purse slung over her arm, sat at the dining table.

"I know how it'll go." She looked at me, her face flushed red like my poinsettias. "I'll be tracking it on our vacation, while you two just go on your merry way."

"Here," I said, extending the spreadsheet toward her. "The shops I assigned to you are in orange. Most of them close between five and six. It's four, so you have time."

She took the paper, stood, and walked to the front entry.

Dad hugged me. "We love you."

I escorted him to the door.

Mom held his overcoat. He took it from her, but she huffed, unhappy about their little spat. Sometimes I didn't know how he put up with her.

"I'll keep you updated if any leads come up, especially with the surveillance videos," I said.

"Good," Mom said. "I want to get my hands on all of them because I'll know who stole it."

Of course, she'd exaggerate her intuition and powers of observation. "They're not going to give you access, so let the professionals do their job," I said.

"That's what you think, but I'm not relenting until I get answers." She opened the door. "I'm sorry for blowing up, but this is my worst nightmare."

"Mine too." I gave her a peck on her cheek.

Chapter 9

The next day, Mom informed me that the detective inquired with Uber and taxi drivers if they drove a customer to any pawnshop on the day of the theft. But none of them stopped by Okie Pawn that afternoon. Nor did the footage reveal anyone from the airport showing up on the pawnshop's surveillance videos.

Mom asked to view the footage from the pawnshop, but the detective denied her request. Mom and I suspected the owner was hiding footage from the parking lot and his office; it didn't make sense not to surveillance those areas. But the detective made it clear the owner had provided all the footage. I wasn't impressed with this man's investigation.

The only positive aspect of this week was talking to Pres. She'd fill me in on wedding planning and her calls to pawnshops; I'd share about the investigation.

So, when she didn't reach out on Wednesday by noon, even though I called and left her a message, I called Moriah and her dad, concerned something happened to her. Neither responded but an hour later, Pres texted that she'd call later.

When six o'clock rolled around and she hadn't called, I imagined her and Ciaran sitting at an Irish pub, eating corned beef and cabbage, laughing about their time at ORU. I didn't want to entertain that scenario, but I couldn't chase it away.

Tempted to text her and Moriah again, I told myself to not stalk them. So, I focused on work, uploading wedding photos to my blog. But by nine, I called her.

"Garrett..." she answered, but I couldn't make out anything else over the pounding music and constant chattering in the background.

"Where are you?" I asked.

"Hold on..." The noises and music gradually became distant. "What did you say?"

"Where are you? It's nine, and you haven't called. Is everything okay?"

"I told you I was going to youth group."

Uh-oh... My throat constricted. I would've remembered if she had told me because I would've wanted to discuss her going, at least to ask if she was attending with Moriah. Did he invite her? Irritated she played off its significance, I snapped at her. "No, you didn't tell me."

"Let's not argue." Her tone was cold. "It probably will go another hour or two. It's rocking here!"

"Why are you there in the first place?" I couldn't hide my irritation.

"Because Moriah and I wanted to check it out. It's exploded since Ciaran's taken over."

I picked up the framed picture of our engagement I kept on my desk. It was my favorite because she was staring into my eyes with longing; I was her world. "Okay, but what does that have to do with you?" I asked, not wanting her to stare at him that way.

"Everything!" She raised her voice. "I can't believe you're threatened by Ciaran when you should be thrilled God's moving among the youth. What's gotten into you?"

I stood as though she had poked me in the side. *Cool your head, Garrett.* But her words stung. I returned the frame to the desk with the picture facing down.

"Did you really hang up?" Pres asked.

"No. I'm frustrated that you forgot about me today." Nausea filled my stomach.

"I'm sorry I didn't call you back." Her voice became gentle. "Trust me, I wanted to, but Mom filled my schedule with an engagement brunch, a staff meeting, then shopping for her mother-of-the-bride gown. I've barely had time to change for tonight."

"Why change?" *Please, not your skinny jeans and tank top.* Blood rushed to my head.

"For comfort. I wanted to get out of my dress pants and ruffled silk top. And teens relate better to adults in jeans and a tee."

I pressed Facetime, wanting to inspect her outfit, but she declined, raising my temperature at least ten degrees.

"Sorry, but I can't Facetime now. It's too distracting. I won't be able to focus on you and the service. Ciaran's about to have an altar call." I formed a fist as she talked. "I promise to call you first thing tomorrow morning."

Jealousy ate at me like a barnacle chewing on a boat's hull. No man wanted to come in second behind an ex. That was material for nightmares.

"Gar Bear, did you hear me?" she asked.

"I don't appreciate you being there with Ciaran. Nor how dismissive you're being. So, do me a favor and don't see him again."

"I'm not Morgan. And I don't care for him that way, anymore, but I don't need to justify myself. I thought you were more mature than this. So, whatever is going on with you, please get it worked out before I fly home."

"I'm not acting petty. You're my fiancée, and I have a right to inquire about him and ask you to not hang out. If no other reason than out of respect."

My heart rate wasn't slowing. Pres and I hardly argued, so I wasn't sure how she'd respond.

"Let's talk about respect," she said. "How about trusting me instead of treating me like a two-timer?"

I gritted my teeth, wondering how charming this Irish dude was.

"I'm getting off this call. We're getting nowhere. Love you," Pres said.

Did she?

I knew she hadn't told me about attending youth group, but I did vaguely recall her talking to her mom about attending when we were at the airport. But with all the drama about the bracelet, I didn't follow through about her attending.

I struggled falling asleep that night, as scenarios of Pres and Ciaran ran through my mind. I tried to tell myself not to worry, but her excitement about youth group, her frustration with my jealousy, and her hardly contacting me all day, overwhelmed my attempts.

Fortunately, she called the next morning. "Hey, babe."

"Did you sleep well?" I asked, trying to find neutral ground.

"Sound. How about you?"

"Not so well. I was struggling about us."

"Moriah talked to me late last night. And if I see it through your lens, I get why you were threatened. But what I was trying to tell you is, you shouldn't worry about Ciaran. I'm engaged to you. And last night, I raved to him about how perfect you are for me."

"Thanks for saying that, baby." Relief spread through my chest. Thankfully, Pres was flying back in four days.

Chapter 10

*A*woke up from a troubling dream. In it, I chased a thirty-something man in a flannel red and green shirt, yelling at him to return the bracelet. As he ran down a dark alley, I got closer to him. But as I extended my hand to grab his shirt, he disappeared. I was facing a red brick wall. I turned to the street and saw my reflection in a six-foot mirror. I was naked and alone.

What did this dream mean? Should I stop pursuing the bracelet and trust God? I needed normalcy and peace. Yet, could I walk away from my guilt? I was an accomplice in losing it, so I was responsible for finding it.

I wrote the dream in my journal then ran three miles.

By late that afternoon as I drove to The Mayo Hotel, my mind wasn't clearer on what direction to take, but I needed to focus on work. As part of my premium photo package, I included a bridal session. It provided not only a more relaxing setting about two months before the wedding, but a practice run for the bride's beauty team. Often, at the reception, the bride would display her favorite image from the shoot. And I usually enjoyed these sessions because as I worked with the bride, she became more comfortable shooting with me.

Today's session was originally scheduled in November, but the bride wanted last-minute alterations on her gown. Now, I had a tight window since we were only three weeks before her New Year's Eve wedding. To edit today's session on time, I'd have to pull an all-nighter tonight or tomorrow.

At the hotel, I pulled into valet parking, waiting behind a black Mercedes. As the valet and bellhop approached the driver, I thought about Gramps. He was a young bellhop here in the late 1930s, hoping to meet celebrities and local dignitaries. Raised in a blue-collar family, he longed to cast a wider social net to "make something of himself."

This was where he met Granny. He said that when she emerged from a white Packard to attend an event, he was a "goner." Although he didn't get her attention that night, he saw her from time to time since she attended many functions as a "socialite" (a term she wouldn't use to refer to herself, but she fit that category since her father was an oil executive).

Built in 1925, the hotel was the epitome of Art Deco extravagance during Tulsa's reign as the "oil capital of the world." The hotel boasted being the tallest building in Oklahoma upon completion. When the economy nosedived in the 1980s, the hotel closed for renovations, but it didn't get a transformation until twenty years later. Since they worked hard to restore many of the original features, I sensed my grandparents' memories living amongst the walls.

I also liked the composition the hotel's exterior provided. Four Doric columns on each side of the double-glass doors composed the ornate, arched front entry with a wrought-iron overhang. Doric columns stood between the arched windows. I'd often shoot couples kissing in front of the entrance, since the background provided symmetry and clean lines.

Looking ahead, the thirty-something guest in a black cashmere overcoat and black leather gloves got out of the car, talking on his phone, not acknowledging the valet and the bellhop nearby.

The bellhop grabbed the man's luggage from the trunk, and then the valet got into the car and drove away.

I pulled up closer to the other valet waiting on the sidewalk. He opened my door then greeted me. "Welcome to The Mayo Hotel," the ginger-haired twenty-something said.

"Thanks. I'm here for a photo shoot. So, I need to grab my equipment first." I handed him a ten in case I'd forget to tip afterwards.

"Appreciate it, sir." He snapped his fingers as he looked at a different bellhop approaching the Jeep. "He's not here overnight."

The bellhop turned and headed inside while I grabbed my camera and light kit.

As I entered the hotel, I thought of how many company Christmas parties I'd photographed here. Dad hired me to shoot these parties and Gramps, serving on the company's board, brought Granny.

Walking past the lobby, I approached the three steps to the Grand Hall. Two five-foot Nutcrackers guarded the bottom step. On the landing, there stood a Christmas tree with silver ornaments. Granny would always stop and admire them. Boy, I really missed her today as signs of her presence surrounded me.

Come on, focus on the shoot.

The event manager placed a sign that read, Space Reserved For An Event, on the marble floor. I waited until she turned to face me, so I wouldn't scare her.

After a cordial greeting, she directed the conversation toward work. "Everything is ready for the session. Feel free to turn lights on or off. The space is reserved until five."

"Thank you," I said.

"I'm off to a meeting. Have fun." She quickly disappeared toward the lobby.

The Grand Hall was a two-story space bordered by floor-to-ceiling beige curtains, columns on the sides, and an imperial staircase in the back. They usually kept the curtains valanced on the columns unless they had an event like today. They were closed on the front and the sides, providing privacy I appreciated, but they left them open at the foot of the staircase.

No one else was here, but I was thirty minutes early. I wanted to set up and test my Speedlites since the bride wanted an ethereal vibe with throw-back glamour—what would happen if an angel hosted a Gatsby soiree.

Strands of pearls entwined with Swarovski crystals ran up the wrought-iron railing. On the landing, a six-foot gold vase filled with towering ivory feathers, white poinsettias, and stems of Swarovski crystals unified the look.

I quickly set up my light kit, carefully metering the room lighting with the flash of my Speedlites to calculate the correct exposure and setting up my gray card to set my white balance correctly.

Then I chilled on a round, high-backed, Art Deco chair. I always termed it the "cow chair" with its brown leather seating wrapping around a six-foot-long, cylinder-shaped white cushion with a black circular pattern and topped with a cascading three-tiered lamp like a wedding cake.

My bride texted. Sorry, the beauty team is almost finished. Will be down shortly.

They were prepping in a suite upstairs.

No worries, I texted.

A notification dinged from my phone's calendar. Call Okie Pawn. I didn't care that the pawn owner escaped the search warrant, I needed to shake him down a little. As I called him, I envisioned him contacting the cops. The last thing I needed was him filing harassment charges on me, especially because he was cozy with the police department. I hung up then stuffed my phone in my pant pocket.

I laid my head on the cow cushion. So unfair I couldn't get what was mine. Great, heartburn crept into my chest. I took a few deep breaths, closed my eyes, and mentally walked through today's session. I'd capture the bride on the landing, in front of the staircase, and a few in the center aisle. I'd lower the exposure to give her that haunting, visceral look.

A quick-talking male interrupted my focus. I opened my eyes and peeked to my left, but I couldn't see him. He must've slipped into the room. Ugh, I'd have to ask him to leave.

"I'm about to meet Celine, so detailed information on the bracelet." The man looked at his watch.

Where have I heard that name recently? A potential client? A past bride?

Once he resumed talking, I stopped wondering about Celine. "She'll want a play-by-play of the bracelet's designer, the type of pearls, and the gems... Seaman Schepps and Akoya pearls. Got it. And citrines, sapphires... Go slower... You know what? Just text all of this."

Was he the broker's nephew? I moved to a chair that provided a clear view of him. He was the owner of the Mercedes, dressed in a tailored navy suit with the initials, JSK, embroidered on his pin-striped cuff. He seemed too high-class to buy jewelry from a pawnshop, but I suppose not if it was his uncle. I've worked with several wealthy clients, and you never knew how they made their money.

"Got your text," he continued, running his hand through his ashen brown hair, stiff like a calcified wave. "No, she was ready to sign the joint tenancy, until her old man planted doubt. I spent an hour fielding her questions about the condo investment, but this will seal the deal... Of course, it's also about business. That's why we work. Oh, hold on." He held the phone away from his ear as he looked at it. "She just texted. I'll be in touch."

What kind of woman was attracted to him?

He stood, tapped the breast of his jacket, and walked with a confident gait toward the front entry. He pushed the curtains aside, and once near the Reserved sign, he extended his arms.

A brunette woman with a blunt-cut bob walked up the three lobby steps. Wearing a tight black pencil skirt and white button-up, she sashayed her hips, sauntering toward him. Yep, that type.

"Hi, baby." The man placed his hands on her back.

They kissed hard; I looked away.

"Ready for your birthday celebration?" he asked.

"Of course," she said placing her hand on his chest.

But instead of presenting the jewelry, he took her hand and led her down the hall to the elevators.

I followed, hoping to catch their names and introduce myself. But the woman pointed farther down the hall and walked toward the ladies' restroom by herself.

He reached into his pants' pocket and grabbed his phone. Then he stared at it like a teenager, his forehead taut and wide, with a stern line running across it. This suit looked like he was one bad deal from a heart attack.

I stood next to him. "Are you from out of town?" I asked.

JSK didn't look up.

"I'm Garrett." I extended my hand. "Great hotel, huh?"

"I'm working," he said, not looking at me.

"No problem, man."

The elevator doors opened. My client emerged in a sequined wedding gown, the wedding planner carrying her short train behind her.

"Garrett," the bride said.

The man glanced at me and then frantically texted something. Could he be the pawnbroker's nephew? I took a step toward him, but Kaylie and the planner headed to the Grand Hall. I needed to focus on the bridal session.

❄

An hour later, as I framed the final shots with the bride—she stood in the center of the aisle with a bouquet of white poinsettias, crystals, and feathers—the elevators opened. The same couple emerged, only they were transformed into old Hollywood style: he in an aubergine velvet blazer, white starched shirt, bowtie, and black trousers; she in a figure-hugging, aubergine gown with a high slit. She wore a black-sequined wrap around her slender shoulders.

As though the fairy godmother had transformed the cold stepsister, this woman's face illuminated like fresh embers. She touched the strand of pearls around her neck as she looked longingly at the imperial staircase. I glanced at the landing, but no one was there. She smiled at something again (not at me or the bride) before leaning closer to her boyfriend.

The couple walked past me, and the woman tugged on the wrap, briefly exposing her wrist. Multi-strand pearls and colored gems radiated. Could it be?

I approached Kaylie. "Excuse me. Could we take a quick break? I need to follow up on something. I promise it won't take long."

"Can you wait a few minutes? We only have this space until five," she said, looking at the wedding planner.

"We can't, Garrett," the planner said. "Our team needs to tear down quickly since the couple for tomorrow's wedding is coming at six for the rehearsal."

"I'll help tear down. Just give me five minutes. I'll explain, but it's urgent. Please."

The bride nodded.

"Five minutes," the wedding planner said.

I pursued the couple as they sauntered to the front entry like they were walking the red carpet. The ginger-haired valet opened the door and then followed them outside. As I opened the heavy glass door, a cool breeze blew. The golden hour cast an angelic glow upon the woman.

Standing about ten feet away, I waited as they stood on the sidewalk. She was on his right as he held her left hand. How she wasn't trembling from the cooler temps was beyond me, but I was grateful she didn't wear a thick overcoat. I needed to spot the bracelet.

As I strained to see her wrist, the sun's rays hit the four strands of pearls on the bracelet. I stepped closer, but the descending sun flashed in my eyes, obscuring my view. As I hooded the light with my hand, her boyfriend covered her wrist and whispered something in her ear. She shook her head, and he leaned away, facing the street.

Needing a closer look, I took short, stealthy steps. "Excuse me," I said.

She turned. "Can I help you?" Her blue eyes were almost translucent, like ice, and her voice soft and familiar. Catching me off guard, I froze for a second.

"Are you okay?" she asked.

"Yes... Have we met?" I drew closer, staring at a perfectly round brown mole above her thin lips.

"No, I've never seen you." She pulled her wrap closer to her bare shoulders.

"Is this man bothering you?" her boyfriend asked.

"No," she said.

"May I see your bracelet?" I stepped so close, her peony and vanilla perfume wafted in the air, reminding me of Granny.

Her boyfriend lightly pushed her to the side, his hand still covering her wrist, and then stepped between us as quick as the Tasmanian Devil. He eyed me from head to foot, probably assessing whether my khaki pants and long-sleeved Scottish flannel met the hotel's nonexistent dress code. "Stop harassing my girlfriend."

"I mean no harm." I raised my hands in the air. "Her bracelet reminded me of the one I lost—well, somcone stole. Belonged to my Granny—"

His eyes flashed red as he extended his hand toward his girlfriend. "Don't show him, Celine. He'll pawn it for drugs."

My mouth gaped at the word "pawn," even more convinced he was the nephew. Before I could respond, she stepped toward the curb's edge, frowned at him, then at me. She was conflicted.

"Seaman Schepps is the designer—" I said.

As he stepped closer, leaving only about an inch between us, his nostrils flared like a bull. "I'll call security if you don't leave us alone."

"You don't intimidate me. I have every right to be here." I pointed to his face.

"I recognize you from the elevators. You were going to snatch my gold watch, weren't you? Jonesing for a high?"

I wanted to punch him. How many times did I fight the stigma of being an addict? He didn't know my history, so I hated his assumption.

"Don't insult me because I don't wear suits." I stood close enough, I could smell his peppermint breath. I looked at his girlfriend. "Ma'am, my bracelet has four strands of Akoya pearls, a gem clasp—"

He shoved my chest hard. I lost my balance and whop! I landed butt-first on the concrete.

"Jordan, what has gotten into you?" the woman asked.

I sprang to my feet and wiped debris from my pants. I rushed toward him and grabbed him by his coat collar. "I know you bought the bracelet at—"

"Valet!" The devil pushed my hands off his velvet jacket then snapped his fingers. "Escort this man inside. He's trying to steal our jewelry."

The ginger-headed valet nodded and set his hand on my arm. "Sir, please follow me."

I jerked my arm free. "I'll walk in by myself."

Another valet drove up in the black Mercedes and parked near the sidewalk. The ginger-haired valet looked at me, then at the couple, uncertain what to do.

"You better open the woman's door," I said.

He straightened his shoulders, approached the couple, and opened the front passenger door. I stared at her wrist, hoping she'd expose the bracelet. As she got into the car, she covered the bracelet with her sequined handbag.

"Sir." The valet driver approached the boyfriend and opened the driver's side door.

"Thank you," the boyfriend said. He didn't tip but got into his car. The valet closed the door and stepped away.

As they drove off, I stared, angry I couldn't see the bracelet clearly. *Wait, the license plate...* I grabbed my phone, but the car turned the corner and disappeared before I could get a picture. I didn't snap the couple either; how would I find them? Were they out-of-town guests? Locals on a staycation?

The photo session! I jogged inside. In the Grand Hall, Kaylie raised her arms and talked quickly to the decor team while the planner was conversing to a young woman by the Reserved sign. I rushed to get everything ready for the shot. Kaylie frowned as she returned to the center aisle.

"I'm sorry. We only have this one pose left. Just relax your shoulders..." I said, but her shoulders remained by her ears.

"I just finished talking to tomorrow's bride. She's irritated we're holding her team back. They're wanting to set up the chairs now for the rehearsal dinner," the wedding planner said.

"Smile, Kaylie," I said.

"I can't focus with everyone staring at me." She turned to face the other bride's décor team.

I got her into this mess, so I better get her out. "How about taking this outside? It's golden hour, so the sun is shining a translucent yellow and orange. It'll create a halo effect on your head, giving you the angelic look you're wanting."

"But the valet and bellhops, not to mention the cars, will impede her," the wedding planner said.

"I'll get them to hold them off."

"Let's go." Kaylie gathered the bottom of her gown. "It's getting too loud in here."

Outside, I paid the valets fifty dollars each to keep the cars at bay. It took another five minutes to get set up as I adjusted the camera settings and put on the lens hood. After I positioned

Kaylie in front of the descending sun, I shot multiple frames to perfect the halo effect I was aiming for. Thankfully, she relaxed, so we could accomplish the mission.

"Look." I approached and then showed her the image on the camera's LCD screen while I cupped my hands to block out the sun.

"Thank you! That's exactly what I wanted." She turned to the planner. "Look." She stepped aside as the planner examined the image.

"Stunning, Garrett," she said.

Yes! Although I was still angry at Jordan, I got a win with Kaylie, probably giving her a much better product than she expected.

Returning inside, Kaylie asked why I had to leave the session abruptly. I explained how I had seen something that resembled my granny's stolen bracelet on someone's wrist. Seizing the opportunity to investigate, I asked the bride and planner if they recognized the couple in the aubergine outfits. The planner had seen the man before at a wedding, but unfortunately, she didn't know him.

After they left, I asked the front desk receptionist and event manager about the couple. The receptionist couldn't divulge their identities, and the event manager said she had seen the woman frequently here but didn't know her.

Awesome! The girlfriend was local.

When I finally got in my car, I rested my hand on the steering wheel. This day couldn't end soon enough. Then Pres called. Hopefully, she'd cheer me up.

"Hi, baby," I said.

"Hey, what are you doing?" she asked, voice strained.

I couldn't handle any more drama. "I finished a bridal photo session, and now I'm headed home."

"Do you have a minute to talk?"

My body tightened. Talk usually meant confront.

"Sure." My tone was flat like a deflated balloon.

"I keep forgetting to ask, but did you confront your mom about disrespecting Dad? She still hasn't apologized."

I laid my head on the steering wheel. *Why today?*

"Babe, did you hear me?" she asked.

"She was voicing an opinion. It wasn't like she insulted his church—"

"Seriously? You don't think she said anything inappropriate, do you?"

I held the phone away from my ears, afraid she'd blast a hole through them. "Calm down. This is getting overblown. I've already assured you I'm available to photograph anything he needs."

"Don't tell me to calm down. I never thought you were a momma's boy until now. But it's becoming clear."

"You want to go there? I've never asked you to apologize to her for losing the bracelet. Because as far as she's concerned, you've managed to lose something that means more than your dad's pride." I grimaced. Until Pres apologized, Mom wouldn't call her dad. Both events seemed impossible.

I didn't know how much time passed, but she didn't say anything for a good minute.

"I knew it! You haven't forgiven me, have you?"

"Of course, I have." I sighed, wishing I hadn't answered the phone. "It was an accident."

"The bracelet doesn't have anything to do with your mom's rudeness. And regarding Dad's pride? Weren't you upset when you thought I disrespected your business?"

Two cars pulled out behind my car, so I was trapped between them. But they both stopped. One driver was applying lipstick, the other was staring at her phone. I honked my horn. I wanted to be home, not stuck in a parking lot going nowhere.

"Say something. I hate when you tune me out," Pres said.

I bit my lower lip, so I wouldn't say something I'd regret. Then I focused on ending this topic.

"Today's not the best day to get into this. I think I saw someone wearing the bracelet. I confronted them and got shoved to the ground. So, if you don't mind, let's talk about this tomorrow. I'll talk to Mom again, but I've got to handle it my way."

"You saw someone wearing the bracelet? When? Where?" she asked with a gentler tone.

Finally, one of the cars drove away, so I eased out, avoiding the car where the woman was still applying her makeup. "During my photo session."

"Do you think it's the bracelet?" Pres asked.

"I think so, but I couldn't get close enough."

As I pulled onto the street, Pres cleared her throat. "I'm sorry about that. I'd be frazzled too. Will you call the police?"

"I don't have enough to go on. That dude would lie and maybe hide it. I don't think it's worth my time, anyway."

"Alright..." Pres's voice raised an octave. "But going back to your mom... Please realize why I'm pushing this. Dad wants assurance I'm marrying into a supportive family."

"I understand." *But did my mom?*

"I better let you go," she said. "I'll talk tomorrow. I love you."

"Love you, too."

This was a horrible day. And when I didn't think it could get worse, it just did.

Chapter 11

Monday couldn't come fast enough. I was swamped over the weekend between staying up nearly all night Friday editing Kaylie's bridal session, then shooting a wedding Saturday evening, and a bridal shower on Sunday afternoon.

Boy, I slept great that night and didn't bother getting out of bed until ten in the morning. I would've slept longer, but I wanted to get ready for Pres flying in. I ran a few miles, got a haircut to impress her, and then by late afternoon, I threw myself into vision planning.

Outside on my patio, I worked on my five- and ten-year goals. While in Vegas, Pres kept reminding me to work on this since she wanted to compare our visions.

In five years, we'd have two kiddos. For passive income, I'd offer an online course on starting a wedding photography business while our family traveled at least three to four months of the year. I'd start shooting wildlife. And she'd speak at women's conferences and write books.

I hoped to transition into wildlife photography in ten years, including shooting for *National Geographic*. I'd show my works at art galleries. We'd establish home bases in Tulsa for six months and Vegas for three—give or take.

I couldn't believe the life we'd live and how compatible we were. All those dreams I imagined as a twenty-something were coming to pass, and I could leave my past behind.

❄

Unfortunately, Pres's flight got delayed, and she wouldn't arrive until after midnight. I didn't get to see her, since she and Moriah caught a ride home with friends who were on the same flight to Tulsa.

Around ten the next morning, Pres came over as I finished making wassail. Today, I wanted to celebrate my ten years of sobriety. Pretty cool. Grandpa and Grandma Bettencourt, Shane, and my best buddy Andrew called to wish me a happy sobriety anniversary. After their calls, I wanted to climb the summit of the Diamond Peak in the Rockies.

I opened my front door. "Hi, babe."

Dressed in a black jogger suit with a hoodie, she caught me off guard. I expected her in leggings and a trendy sweater. If she wasn't called to vocational ministry, she'd have been a fashion blogger. The black bags under the eyes made it look like she had pulled an all-nighter. *Should I be worried?*

"Are you all right?" I asked, taking her black satchel.

"Exhausted from the late flights." She walked inside. "I got us cinnamon rolls at Antoinette's."

"You know what I need." Ever since Vegas, she didn't seem to care about getting fit for the wedding. I preferred this, so she wouldn't get overly stressed with planning.

Once I got settled in the sectional, with her coffee, my wassail, and cinnamon rolls on the coffee table, I patted the empty seat next to me. "Come join me, baby."

She was flipping through her cream Day-Timer.

"Did you hear me?" I asked.

"Coming." She nestled beside me; her legs folded underneath her butt.

I put my arm across her shoulder as I lingered in the light floral scent of her perfume.

"Did you do any vision casting?" she asked, a horse out of the gate.

"I jotted thoughts down."

"How about you read them?"

I grabbed my journal on the side table, opened to the back page, then read it out loud.

Once I finished, I smiled wide. But she frowned. What did I say wrong?

"What the heck? There's nothing about church." She held her arms out.

"Be patient." I tapped her leg. "I'll read the ten-year."

After reciting the items, I shut the journal. I was proud of how I incorporated the church, especially her ministry, into my life plan.

"Have you given any thought to helping the media team?" she asked, coolly.

"I'm available anytime. Just give me three days out there, and I'll capture anything you need."

"Thanks. I'll read my plan." She opened the Day-Timer. On a laminated sheet of paper, she had a printed list with bullet points.

- *Have a baby on year 5.*
- *Help Dad with expansion as they add more satellite churches.*
- *Mentor female teens and young adults.*
- *Live in Vegas for 8-10 months, Tulsa 2-4 months.*
- *Have rental investments for passive income.*

As she expanded the list, my head spun when she mentioned Vegas and rental investments. I asked about her ten-year plan, hoping she'd use the investment to fund our travels. I'd go all-in to leverage money for freedom.

- *Two kids.*
- *Head the women's ministry with 3-5 satellite churches.*
- *Help Garrett oversee the church's media department.*
- *Travel with Garrett when he's shooting wildlife.*
- *Speak at our church's conferences.*

"Wait, I thought you wanted to travel and speak at women's conferences. And write books," I said. "Are you sure you wouldn't get pigeonholed at your dad's church?"

"About that." She gazed into my eyes. "When I was in Vegas, God revealed a lot about *us*. That spiritual gifts assessment showed that my strengths are in administration and leadership. This lines up with a prophetic word I received a few months ago. Someone said they saw me raising up the next generation of women. While I could do that through conferences, I want to stay rooted in a home church and mentor young women."

No, no, no... We couldn't ground ourselves at an expanding church. How could I reconcile that with traveling? "But you can mentor the next generation through your books and speaking engagements. By traveling, you can reach more people."

"I want to live in Vegas full-time. Travel only two to three months a year. Dad's church is expanding, so I want to help Mom with the women's ministry, especially as they open new campuses."

"You can administrate virtually." I pulled my arms to my side, giving us space.

"Gar Bear, of all people, you know how I need to connect in person. Virtual is good, but only occasionally. It's about building relationships."

I contemplated this crossroad. I didn't want to make the same mistake I made with Morgan. I never assured her that we were traveling on the same path.

"What are you thinking?" she asked, running her hands through my hair.

I waited a few seconds; her soft touch soothed me. Yet, I needed to address our visions. "Could you stop massaging my scalp?" I asked. "I like it, but I can't focus."

She put her hands on the Day-Timer.

"Thanks." I closed my eyes, trying to envision a new path, but I only saw two separate ones. Nope, it was premature to panic. "I'm reframing our lives, but I'm confused. We had talked about staying in Tulsa and growing with Believers Church..." *That's it!* Our paths would overlap. While some parts wouldn't align perfectly, we could still travel together.

"I'm sorry, but—" Pres blurted in a tighter pitch than I expected.

I opened my eyes. "Please, let me finish." She looked at her hands if avoiding eye contact. "Look at me, babe." She raised her glance. "My first calling is to us. Where we are and what church we call home aren't as significant as us being a family. If Vegas is where we're called, we'll make it work."

"But would you be satisfied?"

I smiled to reinforce my words. "If you're with me, I will be."

"Are you sure?" She shook her head. "Think about all the traveling you expect to do in the next five to ten years."

"I'll adjust my plans to accommodate yours. My first calling as your husband is to support yours."

She stood. "But... oh... Dad... why did you say that? I..." Tears rolled down her face, cheeks glistening under the soft light from the overhead fan.

"What's wrong?" I stood and embraced her in a bear hug to console her even though I didn't understand why she was crying.

She shot me a surprised glance. "My dad asked me something when I was home. I tried to answer his question, but he was right..."

I shook my head. "About what?"

"He asked if I could conceive myself attending art galleries of your work. Camping with you in the wilderness as you captured wildlife. And not having you available on weekends."

"And...?" Where was she going with this?

"I told him, of course. But it's dawning on me what he meant. I'm incompatible for you and would hold you back. You'd focus more on helping me reach my dreams and not enough on yours. You need a woman with an artistic bent."

Oh God, I couldn't lose her! You brought us together, so she needed to see how we were meant to be... I had to show her.

"Don't forget God brought us together at the right time, so he knew we'd have to trust him to make it work. But that's his genius! Through our different strengths and gifts, we complement each other."

She lightly pushed away from me and put her hands on the sides of her head to think or quiet nagging voices.

"Baby." I touched her chin and tilted it toward me. "We can reach more people. What's important is, we share similar values and want to help each other reach our potential."

"Everything is happening too fast. I can't think. In Vegas, I was happy. I knew what I wanted. But now, as I look at you, I'm confused!"

Her eyes became grey as a vein on her forehead poked out like a tree branch.

"Babe, sit back down." She wouldn't budge. So, I kept my hands on her back and continued talking. "Michigan is coming at the right time. Life will get slower, and you'll see how right we are. And it doesn't matter if we live in Vegas or Tulsa, as long as we will be happy."

"I need to live in Vegas."

I considered Ciaran, and although my anxiety increased, I forced myself to stay calm. "Did visiting with Ciaran resurrect those expectations from ORU? You two one day inheriting your dad's church?"

She paused. "I'm sure it appears that I'm influenced by him, but I'm not. This is about us. What I envision for *our* future."

"Exactly!" I took her hands and held them. "We can live in Vegas eventually and make it work."

She wrenched her hands out of my grasp with a strength she hadn't demonstrated before. "I'm so confused!"

I couldn't move as I watched her go to the dining room and grab her purse. She didn't look at me as she talked. "I need to get somewhere to think."

I glanced at the empty wall where Granny's picture had been. Everything was empty and bleak.

She walked to the entry, just as I realized she was leaving. I rushed toward the front door and stood in front of her. "We can work it out on Christmas break. A lot has come at us suddenly." I extended my hand but only grasped air as she kept her hands along her side.

"Goodbye, love," she said weakly.

I kissed her weak lips, and within a few seconds, she pulled away in silence.

"I love you, Pres." I touched her shoulder.

"I love you, too." She wrung her hands as she waited for me to open the door. She left without looking back at me. The wind blew loud on my face as I stood and watched her drive away.

Inside, I walked to the sectional. On the coffee table, I noticed her mug with her red lipstick marking the rim, her cinnamon roll barely touched.

I needed to go outside where I could think and not get distracted by signs of her leaving.

On my patio, I struggled to catch my breath. Everything tightened. I couldn't lose her! I closed my eyes to focus... What could prove to her that we were compatible?

After some time passed, and my anxiety cleared, I jotted a strategy in my journal.

Volunteer on media team. Meet with her pops about supporting church's expansion. Shoot wildlife 1-2 times/year.

I grabbed my phone to text about when we could meet, but as I dictated the words, she called.

"I... got off phone... Dad—" If the distress in her voice was a six earlier, it accelerated now to a ten.

I had to intervene and show her the light. "Good! I want to meet with him and see how I can help with their expansion—"

"Please, please... I need to focus... get my thoughts out... Can't." That last sentence was muffled. I held my breath, wondering what she'd say. "I'll get this together..." But she sputtered like a stalled car. "I'll call you back. Don't call me." *Click.*

I stood and knocked my journal off the table. I bent to pick it up from the ground and as I stood, I bumped my head. Gah! That hurt! But there wasn't time for pain. I grabbed my phone but didn't know if I should call her dad or text her.

Both were precarious choices, but it'd be best to deal with her first. I texted her my new steps, emphasizing asking her dad about helping the church's expansion. I needed to give her clarity.

Time dragged. It seemed like an hour, but according to my phone, only fifteen minutes had expired.

When she finally called, I answered on the first ring. "Baby," I said. "Did you read my text?"

"Yes, and it reinforced what Dad said. When I had told him what you expect in the future for *us*, he was concerned you'll compromise what you want for *me*..." I heard a stifled sob, then faint clearing of her throat. She continued. "And that will come back to bite us both. We need to be with people who are running on the same path. I don't want to say this! I can't!"

"Wait, what?" I didn't know who I was angrier with: her dad for swaying her away with a subtle tactic, my mom for turning him away from us, or Ciaran for painting a picture of life with him.

"I'm calling off our engagement..." More stifled sobs. "I'm sooo sorry. I love you." *Click*.

I blanked out. My body, my mind, and my emotions were numb. I couldn't sense the wind on my face. The sun glared overhead through thin clouds, but everything looked noir grey as if I was suspended between the conscious and subconscious.

Caw, caw, caw... a crow landed on the patio railing. I waved my hand to scare him away, but he didn't move. His presence jerked me back to reality.

I had to do something, but what? Drive to her house and beg her to change her mind. Call her dad and inform him how wrong he was. Call Mom and tear into her for her pride. But all those options required energy I didn't have.

I needed something to drown out Pres's voice. Her father's. My mother's.

Chapter 12

It was noon, but I didn't want anything to eat. As I started my Jeep, a voice in my head shrilled. *Don't flush ten years of sobriety down the toilet.*

I yelled back, "Don't worry. I just need enough to forget."

I drove to the liquor store and bought a bottle of vodka. That voice echoed: *You can make it without this crutch. Learn to heal from pain.*

"Right! But that won't bring her back, will it?" I pointed toward the window, attacking the air.

At home, I locked the front door and pulled down the blackout shades. I poured the clear liquid into a shot glass. I turned off all the lights except a table lamp then sat on the sectional with my liquor. When I raised the drink to my lips, I looked around, expecting someone to turn on the lights and snatch the shot out of my hand. But no one was here.

Ding! I jumped. I couldn't answer my door. *Ding*!

I remained still. No more dings. What a relief. Once my heart quit racing, I slowly raised the drink to my lips since my hand trembled. Shame enveloped me, but I needed something to cut the edge off this pain.

Ring. My phone lay on the coffee table like an omen. It was Dad. Scrambling to turn it off, I accidentally pressed answer and dropped the shot glass. It fell onto the hand-knotted rug. Vodka spilled onto my warm foot, releasing a tickling sensation. I jerked my foot away.

"Son, it's Dad..." was all I could hear. So I pressed the speakerphone.

"Dad?"

"Are you working?" he asked casually.

"No..." I looked around, paranoid as if eyes were watching.

"Can I come in?"

I caught the grey shadows of the clear bottle on the kitchen counter. "No!"

"Sorry." Dad's voice became soft. "Did I catch you at a bad time?"

I clenched my fists, wanting to be left alone. "Hold on." I stood, needing to hide the mini bottle before letting him in. *Crunch*! The shot glass shattered under my left foot. Shooting pain extended up my leg as I fell against the back of the sectional.

"Ugh!" I bit my lip so I wouldn't scare him.

"Garrett! What's going on?"

"I stepped on glass. Give me a moment."

Click... The door opened; Dad entered. Standing like a camp counselor, he flipped on the overhead light. I squinted, partially covering my eyes as they acclimated to the white light filling the room.

"I asked you to wait." I winced, not wanting to sound so sharp.

"You scared me," he said, eyes locked on mine.

Wanting to distract him, so I could hide the bottle, I pointed to the entry closet. "Hey, how about grabbing cleaning supplies for me?"

I stood, using the sectional as support, and hobbled to the kitchen, not putting weight on my left foot. The shards of glass pierced through the layers of skin. Blood oozed onto the rug and hardwood floor, leaving a trail of red blots behind me.

"You need to stay put. I'll clean this up." Dad walked to the closet.

"I'm good. If you'd retrieve the broom, vacuum, and carpet cleaner..." I grabbed the bottle and stared at it like it was a siren luring sailors. I wanted a drink so bad. "You'll have to reach deep into the closet to find the... You know what? How about going to the garage and grabbing the Shop Vac?"

The detached garage sat at the back of the house since they constructed most of these older homes before the 1950s.

"Let me grab all I can from here," Dad said. "Then I'll get the vacuum."

"Thanks. Just put the cleaning supplies on the dining room table. And I'll clean up my mess."

Keeping the kitchen light off, I quietly grabbed the liquor bottle and placed it under the sink cabinet behind the dishwasher tablets. *Clink, clink, clink.* The bottle banged against the side of the cabinet as I struggled to carefully set it down, while balancing on one foot. Sweat rolled down my face. I looked up, but Dad was occupied in the closet.

Now I needed to get him outside, while I cleaned up the blood.

"Son." He turned on the overhead light over the sink.

I jumped as he stood on the other end of the counter. My stomach tightened as his eyes probed like a flashlight.

"What's going on?" His tone was slightly heightened.

"Nothing." I reached down and picked the shards of glass out of my foot as warm blood trickled on my hand.

"Son, I saw the vodka."

As I retrieved a first-aid kit from the sink cabinet, I considered a plausible alibi.

"Let me wrap that." Dad grabbed the kit from me and then draped my arm around his shoulder. "Come sit on the barstool." He helped me onto the stool at the kitchen island. As he bandaged my foot in silence, shards of shame dug deeper into me than the broken pieces of glass.

Dad stood. "That should be good. When was your last tetanus shot?"

"A few years ago." I wanted to be alone. "Thanks, Dad. I've got it from here."

"I'll get the Shop Vac from the garage." He disappeared toward my mudroom.

While I waited, I thought about my sobriety journey. Most of the time, Dad was so patient and when he got frustrated or angry, he explained how my pain hurt him. His transparency disarmed me, so I shared how difficult it was to stay sober. I never wanted to put him through that again, yet I didn't want to face this agony.

Screech... The back door opened. Dad carried the Shop Vac in. Once he was in the living room, he spoke. "I'm not letting you do this alone."

We cleaned the mess. He carefully swept and vacuumed the glass, while I rubbed, blotted, and dabbed blood off the area rug, hardwood floors, and sectional. Every movement taxed my muscles as Pres's words hovered like careless vultures.

I'm calling off our engagement... I rubbed harder as her words kept repeating in my mind until my hands were raw.

Once I finished, a large spot of turquoise blue on my favorite area rug faded into a pale hue. I took it easier on the hardwood floor and sectional. By the time the traces of blood were gone, my body dripped with warm sweat.

"Mind giving me time to jump in the shower?" I asked.

"I'll grab lunch," he said.

I took my time as the lukewarm shower sobered me. When I came out to the living room, Dad had burgers on the island counter. Food would help quell this desire for something.

We sat at the kitchen island. His presence comforted me, but I looked down. "Pres called off our engagement." Hearing those words come out of my mouth was different than hearing them from Pres's. With her, I was too numb to think, but now, the words were weights sinking me to the abyss. I didn't need anything else. I didn't want anything else. Nothing else mattered.

"What?" Dad's eyes became big. "Really? I'm sorry. When?"

"This morning. Something about how we're incompatible... I'd sacrifice for her at the cost of my career. I don't know. It's all fuzzy, like it didn't happen."

Dad drew me into a bear hug. I cried soft tears. *Why wasn't I enough?*

As he pulled away, he patted my back. "Eat before it gets cold." I waved my fingers, so we could focus on something else.

He chuckled. "Always thinking of others."

We sat at the island counter. Dad said a brief prayer then bit into his burger while I guzzled the chocolate milkshake. Sugar was my drug of choice today.

Once we finished eating, he retrieved a white gift bag from the console table near the entry.

"What's that?" I asked. In my haze earlier, I hadn't noticed he brought a gift.

"For your ten-year sobriety anniversary." He handed it to me. "I figured you and Pres... Sorry..." He crinkled his nose.

I swallowed the lump in my throat. Talk about the worst timing to call off our engagement. But I needed to distract myself, so I pulled a long, narrow wooden jewelry box out of the bag with the initials CWD carved in the center. Lifting the hinged top, I stared at a thin, silver cross necklace.

"It belonged to Gramps," Dad said. "He wore it most of his adult life. Then, when your mom and I were having marital troubles, he gifted it to me. It's time you have it."

I handed him the wooden box. "As much as I cherish this, I don't deserve to keep anything else that belongs to them."

He shook his head. "*You* didn't lose the bracelet. And even if you had, it's not about worth. This necklace is a reminder of the battle you fought and won."

Yeah, and lost again.

"Like you, I didn't consider myself worthy of his necklace, but it served as a reminder why I was valuable to the family and to Mom. It taught me to fight for us even when I wanted to quit. Trust me, I was ready to throw in the towel, but knowing what Gramps and Granny endured in their marriage, this cross served as a beacon of hope."

"So, this saved you and Mom?" I was skeptical this token could resolve years of marital issues.

"It was a reminder to fight."

"I need it then." I lifted the necklace out of the box and held it in my palm.

"Gramps understood why addiction is so tempting. He had buddies who couldn't integrate into civilian life after the war. A few committed suicide while others ruined their lives with alcohol and drugs. He got close to succumbing to the bottle himself when nightmares haunted him, but he had a stronger yes." Dad's hazel eyes were serene, like a steady stream.

"Hmm..." My *yes* just walked out the door today.

"During the war, Gramps befriended a medic who was also from Oklahoma. They had girls back home. One day, the medic heard from a relative that his fiancée wouldn't wait for him and married someone else. Lousy thing to do to a soldier in war."

I looked away.

"Should I continue?" Dad tilted his head toward me.

I forced a smile. "Yeah."

"The young man was heartbroken. He told Gramps the necklace was his reminder that God would keep him safe, so he could return home and marry his fiancée. After the news, the medic made Gramps promise that if anything happened to him, Gramps would wear it. Gramps noticed the medic took more risks as he dragged wounded men off the battlefield.

"One day, a young soldier got his foot stuck in a hole and couldn't get out. Seeing the lightning of gunfire, the medic ran to the soldier and covered his body. He stayed until Gramps and a few other soldiers rescued them."

"Gramps was quite a soldier." My respect for him grew.

"Yep." Dad continued the story. "The medic died from gunshot wounds while the rescued soldier was unscathed. Gramps wore the necklace every day, as a reminder to make something of his life to honor the medic. But it's as endearing how Granny stuck by him even when it became difficult."

Gramps was a congenial fellow, but he didn't have patience like Granny. I'd cringe when he'd yell at her then apologize nearly in tears. Or he'd walk away, hanging his head as he muttered something. One time, he walked by after he argued with her. He didn't acknowledge me but caressed his chest. The necklace must've been underneath his shirt. I knew he had suffered something traumatic, but I didn't know what.

He never dwelled on anything melancholy for too long in front of us but would break into a joke or a lighthearted vignette. His irreverence and dismissive manner used to bother me, but I realized now it was his coping mechanism.

I freed the cross out of the box to examine it, catching my reflection in its newly polished surface.

"Put it on and check if it's the length you like," Dad said. "I replaced the old chain."

I secured it around my neck and positioned it underneath my T-shirt. It came to my upper chest. "The length is good."

"Don't you want to wear it on the outside of your shirt?"

"No, it's protected this way." I wasn't going to take a chance of losing it.

After he left, I poured the liquor down the toilet and threw the empty bottle in the trash cart outside. I turned my phone off for the rest of the day in case Mom would call.

CHAPTER 13

That night as I got ready for bed, I listened to holiday tunes. When "Jingle Bells" came on, I envisioned Pres and me laughing and sledding on the snowcapped hills. It sowed a seed of hope that Pres would come to her senses, and we'd get back together.

The next morning, I turned on my phone, with slight anticipation Pres had called. But instead of hearing her voice, I was reminded of Mom's calls, voicemails, and texts from yesterday. I wanted to roll back in bed, but I had a mountain of work facing me.

As I got ready, I listened to Mom's messages. As I expected, she ranted about how she couldn't believe Pres called off the engagement. Because she couldn't wring all her anger in one message, she left another a few hours later, raving about Pres's timing: *Who ends a relationship just before Christmas?* And another asking if there was anything she could do.

By seven, she sent a barrage of texts: Are you okay? Would you please call? Thankful Michigan is coming soon. We'll be there to support you through this. I love you!

As much as the holiday songs resonated childhood sentiment, Mom's messages recalled childhood dread. How could I spend a week under the same roof? The agony of her sympathy, mixed with her offense with Pres, would be insufferable.

Although I looked forward to a getaway, I couldn't put up with Mom right now. I'd wait until I could tell her in person. She needed to experience my resolve. So, I didn't respond.

When Moriah arrived at nine, I could focus on her and work. But as she entered the house, I didn't think about anything but Pres. Did she talk to Moriah about calling off the engagement?

Was she expressing remorse? Was she willing to meet with me to talk it over maturely?

She hugged me, "How are you, boss?"

"Hanging in there, I suppose." Why did Pres call it off? Why before we had premarital counseling? Before talking through our expectations? It didn't make sense.

"Can I fix you something?" she asked. "Coffee? Herbal tea? Water?"

Was she serving me in my home? "What's going on?" I asked, hoping a leading question might inspire her to open up about Pres. I didn't want to come across as pathetic or weak.

"You haven't told me if you want something," Moriah said.

"It's my home. What do *you* want?"

"Sorry. I'm... well..." She sat at the table, put the backpack on her lap, and pounded on the canvas material like a funeral march.

I walked into my kitchen. "I've got chamomile tea unless you want something stronger, like black."

She turned to face me, grimacing, "Black works."

Once I fixed us tea, I sat next to her. Now would be a good time to find out more about Pres and Vegas.

"Thanks. I've got some things from Pres. Where do you want me to put them?" She held up a green backpack.

"Here." I shoved the spreadsheet of pawnshops and dates when I called or visited them to the far end of the table, making space in the center.

I doubted Pres was calling pawnshops now. How convenient for her, even though she lost the bracelet. Seemed like that was how my ex-girlfriends did. They left a mess for me to clean up.

As if going through a deceased person's home, Moriah arranged the items on the table. One by one—things that belonged to me, which I had left with Pres. The neck scarf she borrowed at Winterfest, a black OSU Cowboys sweatshirt with orange lettering folded neatly, and a Scottish plaid button-up she borrowed for her dad when he had visited over Thanksgiving. All of it mocked me as they were tied to our dates. I always liked her wearing my clothes as a reminder we were together.

Moriah touched my arm, and I jumped a little, as I was lost in grief. "How are you holding up, boss?"

I shrugged, not knowing what to say.

"I hate doing this, but here..." She placed a brown, hard-cased ring box on the table away from the clothes. The same box that fell out of my hands and rolled underneath Mom's armchair. I stared like there was a bomb inside. "The only reason I brought it over today is..." Moriah bit her lower lip, hesitating to break the bad news too quickly. "She hoped you could recoup your money."

I grimaced. That wasn't what a man wanted to hear.

"I'm sorry," Moriah said.

"She thought of everything, didn't she?" My hand trembled.

"She's cleaning out the apartment since she's moving to Vegas *this* weekend."

"Oh." That was a harder gut punch than the clothes and the ring. Was Pres erasing all memories of our time together?

"It's not about you; she's escaping a lot of stress right now. She's not herself but making rash decisions."

I stood and talked as if seeing Pres. "It's Dad and Ciaran, isn't it? They talked you into moving back, painted a picture of how they need you in Vegas, and how I'm not right for you."

Moriah stepped closer to me. "How about going up to the office?"

Nodding, I became robotic, following her upstairs. She sat at an oak wood round table near the center. I went to my desk, where I faced the glass doors leading to a second-story balcony over the backyard. The view was a selling feature that lured me to buy this place. I enjoyed listening to northern mockingbirds, finches, and swallows as I worked. Hopefully, nature and work could anesthetize my pain.

I still needed something soothing, so I glanced near my laptop where two framed pictures stood: one I took in the Rockies and another of Skye, my childhood lab.

All right, let's get work done.

While we worked, scheduling meetings with prospective brides, I edited photos. Moriah uploaded the finished photos on our blog and posted them on my social accounts. I asked about her Christmas plans. She hesitated to say but informed me she was spending it at her parents' in Ohio. I coaxed her to disclose that her boyfriend would join them, and they'd go skiing, snowmobiling, and snowshoeing. All the things I planned to do with Pres in Michigan.

Glancing at the gallery of wedding photos on the right wall, I gripped my pen tight. All the couples with eyes locked onto each other's. It was simple arithmetic, right? First, you dated, second, became engaged, and third, got married. So, why couldn't I solve this math problem?

After hours of meaningful work, when the sun started descending and Moriah would soon be leaving, I got the burning question off my chest. "What happened in Vegas?"

"What do you mean?"

"Pres calling off the engagement."

She pressed her hands in front of her. "All I can say is she's been going a hundred miles per hour. Losing the bracelet and not finding a wedding gown upset her. And when she returned home, she realized the church here is focused on growing small groups, not on expanding to new locations. All that added to her stress. And we know how she makes rash decisions when overstimulated." She paused. "Give her time and see what God does."

Ding! Ding! Who could be here? I still held out hope that Pres would show up. I excused myself to answer the door.

I rushed downstairs, turned on the porch light, and looked through the peephole. Mom held a to-go bag from Weber's, a local burger joint. I glanced at the clock in the entry. It was already five-thirty. Where did the time go?

Setting my head upon the entry wall, I didn't want to answer. But if I didn't, she'd only return later, a bounty hunter pursuing a fugitive. I opened the front door.

"Thank God, you're home. I've been worried about you." Mom entered then hugged me tight.

I pulled away, still blaming her for offending Pres's dad. "Moriah and I are working."

"It's good timing then. She's probably about to leave."

What I wanted to say was, *No, I want you to leave.* But Mom walked into the kitchen and put the food on the counter with a determination to make my life easier. I didn't want to fight with her tonight.

I glanced at the ring on the dining table. Not wanting to get Mom heated about Pres, I grabbed the ring box and went to my bedroom. It took me a few minutes to decide where to hide it, so I wouldn't see it. After a brief debate, I put it in my bottom drawer with the ties and other accessories.

When I returned to the dining room, Mom was moving the pile of clothes from the table to the sectional. She had already put my papers in an orderly pile in my basket like Pres would do.

I looked away, as though Pres was here. Why did I answer the door?

Standing with my hands in my jeans, I glanced at the floor. I didn't want Mom around right now, so what could make her want to leave? Christmas vacation popped in my head. "I can't make Michigan."

"What?" Mom's hand waved to dismiss my announcement. "Don't be ridiculous. It'll be good for you to get away. Everything here will remind you of her. Now, sit and eat."

"I need to stay here and catch up on work." I sat in my chair while Mom retrieved the food and set it on the table.

"Having family around will help, even if you don't want to attend Caroline's wedding. Everyone will understand," she said. "If you're concerned about Uncle Earl and the bracelet, Caroline is wearing Granny's pearl-drop earrings."

"Is he still mad?" I hung my head, ashamed that because of me, Caroline couldn't wear the bracelet. When would this nightmare end?

"I informed him you're a responsible young man, and just because you're not married, it doesn't make you irresponsible—" Mom covered her mouth.

"So, you told him we broke up?" I asked, irritated Mom already aired my news on the street. Why not take out an ad? *Hey, my thirty-something son is single. Taking applications from chaste woman in Tulsa.*

"Sorry. It was just more to defend you, so he'd understand you're going through a lot right now."

"Next time, don't speak for me. It was my news to tell. And I don't need you protecting me, either. I can handle Uncle Earl."

"I'll keep that in mind." Mom tilted her head, still concerned for my well-being.

"If you need to work, why don't you stay with us for a few days? Dad will set you up in his office. I'll cook and wash your clothes. Make it easier to work all day." She touched my elbow, but I pushed her hand away.

"No, I don't need you to take care of me."

"Don't be ugly—"

"Hi, Mrs. B." Moriah walked into the dining room. Did she hear Mom?

"Hello, Moriah. Lovely to see you." Mom waxed on her camera smile, wide with lips shut.

I stood.

"I'm leaving, Garrett," Moriah said. "Don't get up."

"No, please stay," Mom said. "Do you want a hamburger or a chicken sandwich?"

Of course, Mom bought extra.

"Moriah, stay," I said, hoping her presence would stop Mom from talking about Pres.

"I'll have the burger, thanks." Moriah sat next to me, for support.

Mom talked about Michigan almost nonstop as we ate. She knew better than to incite my anger by asking probing questions about Pres. I didn't want to hear about all the fun activities we'd do in Michigan, knowing it was her way of trying to change my mind, but that was the safer of the two topics. Moriah asked about our family's Christmas traditions and favorite holiday recipes, so I ate in silence, grateful she was a buffer.

Once we finished eating, I needed to let Mom know her tactic didn't work. "Moriah's going home for Christmas break. I ordered her to not work that week, so she can take time off. Another reason I need to stay in Tulsa."

"Fortunately, Lauren's decent on social media, so you will have help in Michigan," Mom said.

"I advised Garrett to post pictures, especially in Stories, of the wedding venue. So cool!" Moriah wasn't helping my case.

"Thank you. I don't want Garrett alone on Christmas. As a family, *we* can look out for him."

I clenched my teeth, angry at Mom's disrespect. "I'll be fine."

As if she could read my thoughts, Moriah nodded in agreement. "That's what you said when you—" Mom's hand shook.

"When what? I don't need a parole officer."

"Don't be impertinent. You know what I mean."

"I'm not desperate." If Dad had told her about the vodka, her panic would've come through the voicemail, grabbed me by the throat, and shook all the temptation (or my patience) out of me.

"She hurt you!" Mom's eyes darkened. "Yes, I'm angry—especially as I look at you. Your complexion is pale, and your eyes are drooping. I know when my son's depressed."

I had enough of her fear. "You're afraid I'll relapse." Although she would've been justified now, I was weary of her always jumping to that conclusion whenever I experienced a major hardship.

"Yes." She covered her mouth not expecting to admit her nightmare.

I said nothing, wishing she'd leave.

"I'm sorry, Moriah," Mom said.

I shot a glance at my assistant. For a moment, I forgot she was here.

"Oh no. It's healthy for you to talk about this." Moriah stood. "I don't need to make it uncomfortable, though."

Sorry," I said. "I'll walk you to the door."

"No, please stay." Mom glared at Moriah as if looking at Pres. "I have a few questions to ask you if you don't mind."

"No, that's not a good idea," I said. "Moriah doesn't know anything about Pres's situation."

Mom stood and faced her. "Don't worry, dear, I only have one question. It's a mother's prerogative."

Moriah gave me the side-eye. "Yes?"

"Do you think it was fair how Presleigh called off the engagement so abruptly?" Mom asked.

Moriah paused. I wanted to step in and tell her to not answer, but Mom would only press harder.

"Fair isn't an accurate description of Pres's actions." She patted Mom's shoulder in a gesture of comradery. She continued though Mom scowled. "While it's not my place to judge her actions, I'd say she's struggling with a lot of moving parts. I'm praying for her."

"Thank you." I looked at Mom. "There's your one question. Now, excuse us as I escort Moriah to her car." I raised my brows to warn Mom to lay off.

"You're a special girl, Moriah. If only Gar—"

"In Ohio, Moriah's spending time with her boyfriend. He seems like a cool guy." I placed my hand on Moriah's back and led her to the front door.

Moriah waved at Mom as we walked past. "It was wonderful to see you, Mrs. B. Enjoy Michigan."

"We will, dear. You enjoy your family." Mom waved back.

Outside, while Moriah and I were alone, I gave her a hug. "Sorry about Mom. She's still upset."

"Don't apologize. It's how moms are, but I'm more concerned about you. Promise you'll go to Michigan and not stay here alone?"

"No can do, but I'll keep you up to speed on work and how I'm doing. Now, you enjoy Ohio."

After Moriah drove off, I went inside to deal with Mom. She was loading the dishwasher.

"Are you trying to piss people off?" I asked, standing next to her.

"She handled my fair question."

"It's not your place to ask her; it's mine. I need you to let me handle my life." I didn't care that my voice accelerated.

"If you had told me these things, I wouldn't need to ask her." She placed a plate inside. "But it hurt you didn't call me but relied on Dad to break the news. What else was I supposed to do, when you didn't bother to answer my calls or texts?"

"I would've explained it all in my timing." I crossed my arms.

"You shouldn't spend Christmas alone."

"Really? I'm a grown man, so stop worrying about me drinking."

She closed the dishwasher. "What if... I don't know, but I wish I couldn't stop seeing you in the ditch or in jail... or like..."

"Like?" Mom was caught in a cycle of fearing the worst. But if she didn't change, I might want to live in Vegas, if Pres and I got back together.

"Shane's brother."

"Seriously? He isolated himself," I said. He was driving drunk and ran into a guardrail at 110 mph. He died instantly. At that time, I was in the throes of outpatient rehab.

"You do not know what I suffered when you drank." Mom clutched her chest. "The nights I stayed up wondering if you'd come home safely after being with your friends. Worried the police would call, saying you've crashed on the interstate."

"You already gave me the gory details during therapy. I can't manage your emotions and mine. I need to return to work."

"Amazing how you open up to Dad but go on silent with me. I'm trying to help."

"I don't need your sympathy." A surge of guilt, resentment, and self-pity rose from my chest.

Mom clutched her hands together. "I need assurance you won't drink. And if you're tempted, call Dad or Shane."

"I will." She knew my addictive tendencies, so that drove her fear. But I'd walked through enough trials; she should trust me.

"Thank you." She kissed my cheek.

Within a few minutes, she left.

The next day, I drove to a meeting with a prospective bride at a coffee shop Pres and I frequented. Memories hit like a Speedlite's flash: spending hours at a coffee shop laughing or playing a board game. Going on a scavenger hunt downtown on our second date. The first kiss after we came dead last, too distracted with getting more acquainted. Pres saying she loved me. In hindsight, her saying that first won my heart, and I was dead set on marrying her.

All those memories reminded me of what I lost and might never get back.

And with the heirloom investigation at a standstill, I had little to keep me here. Mom had called the detective and reported my incident with Jordan. But the detective made it clear that unless there was more evidence, there wasn't much he could do. And they already assigned him to another case. He advised us if the bracelet showed up in the database, he'd let us know.

I had to escape this city. I texted Dad that I'd be coming to Michigan.

Chapter 14

Since we didn't make it to Michigan until late into the night, I slept in as long as I could, longer than the rest of the family. A stream of light beaming through the window and my phone dinging woke me up. But it sure beat the city sirens rushing past or the honking of a car.

Mom texted: Dad and I are headed to the grocery store. Lauren and Shane are at his parents. Your breakfast is warming in the stove. We'll be home by 11.

Sweet news! I'd explore the property in solitude. First, I needed to get caffeine and nourishment. Downstairs in the spacious kitchen, I made a fresh pot of coffee and, as it brewed, I walked around the vacation rental. A wood sign with a roll of brown paper displayed a handwritten message: *Welcome, Bettencourts! Thanks for celebrating Christmas here.* I took a picture with my camera phone then posted it on my Stories.

While I preferred the log cabin style, the modern farmhouse was warm and inviting. They pulled off the vintage look with a pot-bellied stove near the front entry, a wood stove in the kitchen, and two rotary phones on a display shelf, juxtaposed with a contemporary vibe: the stainless-steel appliances, barista-style coffee station, and two wrought-iron railing staircases. And with a festive cap, a ten-foot Christmas tree stood by the rock fireplace and a baby grand piano.

After I enjoyed a cup of coffee and hearty servings of breakfast casserole, I snagged a chocolate-covered pretzel rod from a chocolate gift basket set on the booth table—a gift from the hosts. Then, dressed in my Oklahoma State University hoodie, flannel-lined jeans, and a long-sleeved tee, I headed outside.

Since it was in the high forties with a less humid climate than Tulsa, I didn't need my thermal jacket or gloves.

Standing on the wraparound porch, I took pictures of the venue. I got a close-up of the large white cross on the two-story barn and of the crab apple tree in front of the farmhouse since it cast a dark silhouette upon the highly reflective snow. I liked how the pops of red on the barn and "clubhouse" facility gave the venue a pristine, clean look among the predominately white landscape of the farmhouse, large shed, and snow.

After approaching the top of the barn, I took shots to post on social. It helped this place was pristine like a brochure. The front entrance had ornate double-paned, cherry wood doors and a wide eave framing the barn. A large red sign with *Sonshine Barn* painted in a white ornate font hung left of the eave.

Ahead, a waving crest of snow-covered hills, still and silent, filled the landscape. The sky was overcast with low-lying fog casting a greyish hue on the thick woods along the horizon. They were probably composed of sugar maples, white birch, hardy oaks, and steady hickories—towering toward the scant clouds. On the edge of the woods, evergreens dotted the hills with their emerald hue, a reminder that life grew in the harshest of seasons.

Yet in the middle of this natural beauty, I couldn't shake off the desire for her. Pres was supposed to be here. Observing all the order of nature, it was difficult to accept the chaos of our relationship. I still struggled with the reality that we weren't together.

To escape my frustration, I headed toward the hills. *Kerplunk!* I slipped on the melting snow and fell on my butt. *Ouch!* I slowly stood and wiped the dingy snow off my jeans.

With my hands bone chilled, I headed to the clubhouse across from the barn. The bottom level of the clubhouse reminded me of an alpine lodge with large stone walls, and red and green wreaths on each window. The top half was red with white trim matching the barn.

Inside, they'd created a glorified man cave, exactly the space where I'd like to get ready on my wedding day. Standing in an open room, I snapped shots of the Pac-Man console, the billiard table, the blue-green couch, and a large flatscreen TV on the wall.

On my left, there was a window overlooking the "basement" floor below. Seriously? The basement level contained a half-court basketball gym with a huge scoreboard. This place was a groom's playground. Although I wasn't on a basketball team in high school, I'd engage in a few pickup games here and there.

My phone dinged; I jumped as it awakened me from my seclusion.

Moriah texted: How are you? Glad you're posting shots of the venue. Followers and potential brides will eat up a winter wonderland Christmas.

I texted her photos of the snow-covered hillside, the front of the barn with the cross, and the basketball court: This place has it all.

Yes, she texted. Also, this gives you an opportunity to promote your wildlife hobby. I'm sure you'll see deer and other animals there.

I gave her a thumbs-up emoji then created a regular post on my feed with three images: the venue from the top of the barn, the rolling snow-covered hills, and the basketball court with the caption: Cool place.

Within thirty seconds, my caption grew: Where else would a wedding photographer spend Christmas vacation but at a wedding venue? What is your favorite shot? Share in comments. Evergreens, snow, and basketball emojis, then #Tulsaweddingphotographer #midwestweddingphotographer #oklahomaphotographer #okbrides #oklahomawedding.

I texted her: You're on vacation. Get used to subpar posts while you're gone. No work, remember?!?

Roger that, she texted back, but use this pattern as a template, please!

I scrolled quickly through my feeds. Pres's came up. She had a carousel of pictures in a post. The first was Pres with her parents on their deck. She looked hot in a grey checkered mini skirt, white tee, and black blazer.

Another one caught my attention. At her dad's church, Pres and her dad stood next to each other in front of the stage, while a strawberry blond dude stood on a step above them. His hands were on Pres's shoulders.

I tapped the photo and tags appeared. Ciaran Houlihan showed up on his face. I clicked on his account. His bio read: From Belfast. Lives in Vegas. Loves Jesus, family, and football.

So, this was the Irish youth pastor. I didn't expect this guy to be rugged, with his slight beard and hair almost touching his shoulders.

I scrolled through his feed: surrounded by youth at her dad's church. The caption: Find your people, find your purpose. Love leading this thriving group of on-fire youth. He had the church's name in hashtags. Another with him playing soccer for some league. (I groaned. Pres played soccer in high school and college.) There was one where he stood with Pres's dad on their deck. The caption got me: Love this man. Helped me through tough times with Mom passing. Why I'm back. Follow the vision!

I looked for a post of him and Pres together, but I couldn't find any. Having seen enough, I exited out of Instagram.

In counseling, I discovered the problem wasn't usually what's on the surface but issues that lingered deeper. Ciaran wasn't the cause of the breakup, but I didn't like how his vision would fit in conveniently with Pres's.

Come on, man. You're meant to be. Push through this!

Needing something to expend my frustration on, I headed downstairs to the regulation half-court basketball space with white inbound lines, the free-throw lines, and the three-point boundaries on the floor.

After I placed my sweatshirt on the bottom step, I grabbed an orange and black ball since it reflected my university colors. I dribbled to the free-throw line and focused on the shot. Just as I released it, Shane arrived.

"Hey, glad I found you," he said, skipping the last step, so he wouldn't trample on my sweatshirt.

Air ball. I turned to face him. "What's up?"

"Want to play?" Shane walked onto the court. He took off his OU sweatshirt and tossed it on top of my OSU sweatshirt.

"Bring it." I retrieved my ball then dribbled to the free-throw line. "First one to score to ten wins."

He countered. "How about twelve since there's a three-point line?"

"Even better." Now was my opportunity to win something.

I dribbled past him, but he stole the ball in one swat. As I turned to guard him, he ran past me and went in for a lay-up.

"Score two-zero." Shane tossed me the ball.

He was quicker and more agile, while I excelled in endurance and upper body strength from hiking, rock climbing, and kayaking. But I was still up for the challenge.

"I'm still warming up," I said.

I dribbled then released a three-point shot. Air ball. He rebounded and ran to the three-point line.

Whoosh! "Five-zero, brother." This time, he thrusted the ball into my hands. I dribbled past him and made the layup. "Five-two."

We went back and forth until the score was ten-four. He posted near the basket. *No, I couldn't get beat.* He faked to the left, but I stayed in position in front of him. He jumped to release an arched shot, so I slammed into his body. The ball went into the air toward the hoop. Whoosh!

He came down hard, landing on his side. I extended my hand, but he shook his head. "Ugh! My arm..."

I hung my head. I was better than this.

He raised his hand, and his wrist went limp. "I might've sprained it."

"Can you lift it by itself?" *Please, don't be broken.*

He grimaced. "Kind of."

"Let's go to the walk-in clinic," I said, wanting to be of service, especially as guilt rose.

"No." He stood but grimaced in pain. "It's all good. I just need to ice it."

"Sorry." I tapped his back. "I was trying to block the shot."

Shane snickered as he headed toward the steps. "You slammed into my body."

"I got carried away, but that's no excuse for fouling hard." I walked to the step and grabbed my sweatshirt, riddled with shame for letting my emotions get the better of me. I had caved into behavior I'd criticize others for—when they let winning reign supreme over a game.

"I'm more concerned about you. From the time we drove here to now, you've been distant."

"It's still hitting me hard." While I didn't want to spend this break with family sympathizing with me, especially Mom and Lauren, Shane was someone who wouldn't dwell long on this—just enough to show he cared.

"Do you know why I married your sister?"

I furrowed my brows. *Where was he going with this?*

"Sorry, I'm not changing the subject," he said.

I smiled. "She has a cool brother?"

"At least you haven't lost your sense of humor." Shane grabbed his sweatshirt with his left hand, tucking it under his arm.

I stopped near the bathrooms as I waited for him to reach the top floor. He winced as he touched the railing on the last step. "On a serious note, I couldn't live without her," he said.

I grabbed a white towel from a basket. This place had thought of everything. I handed one to him since we were dripping with sweat.

"That's why I want to marry Pres." I wiped my forehead with the towel. "Being in Michigan is reinforcing how much I miss her and can't do life without her."

Shane wiped his face and forehead with his left hand. I hoped he didn't break his wrist.

"Before Lauren," he said, acting unconcerned about the injury, "I was seeing this gal on and off for five years. We almost got engaged, but she decided she'd serve overseas on the mission field."

"Oh, I never knew this. So, you didn't want to follow, huh?"

"I struggled to decide if that was the life I wanted. We connected over being missionary kids as we understood each other's unconventional childhoods. But once I became friends with Lauren, I tapped into a passion that once served as a wound. Then, what I needed to do became clear."

Shane walked into the living area and sat in an armchair.

"What passion?" I tossed the towel into the hamper.

"Financing and promoting charitable organizations, especially missionaries."

"Lauren is zealous about that, too."

Shane grimaced and then clutched his wrist. At least it didn't look swollen. "A major pain as a missionary kid was how supporters forgot about us on the mission field. If the US economy took a downturn, supporters cut off funding without blinking an eye. So, we'd struggle to make ends meet. Wasn't like we could get a decent-paying job in Nigeria." He shook his head. "There's nothing worse than feeling abandoned overseas. I'd get riled up, much more than my sister and my parents would."

"What did your girlfriend say about this decision?" I asked.

"She thought I was trying to convince her to not go overseas. It was a tough couple of months. Once I made that decision, my mind became clearer as I realized what connected us wasn't enough to hold us together."

I crossed my left leg over my right and leaned against the wall. "I've never met a woman I could connect with on such a deep level like Pres. We enjoy learning and supporting each other's passions. And hey, she looks hot in yoga pants. That should count for something, right?"

I laughed, trying to run from the fear of Pres and me not getting back together.

He shrugged. "Who's that woman you can go into battle with?"

"I've found her." Wanting to change the subject, I approached him. "I'm here if you need to go to urgent care."

"Nah, I'll be fine." He headed to the door.

Fouling Shane hard was a wake-up call, reminding me too much of my drinking days. I couldn't see how my behavior affected others, especially my family. So, I blamed them for much of my pain. Ironically, that caused a cycle of pain as I continued to hurt them. I ran harder into my addiction, as shame piled onto the burden of emotions I tried to ignore.

Chapter 15

When I woke up from a nap, Shane's anecdote lingered in my head. I wanted to believe Pres and I were headed in the same direction. So, I sat at the desk and jotted a strategy in my journal using bullet points like Pres did:

Operation Pres:

- *Contact Cheryl, the wedding planner. Ask if she'd add me as a preferred vendor.*
- *Text images of MI.*
- *Shoot photos & work the book table at women's conferences.*

I WIN!!!

I emailed Cheryl. For the first time since arriving in Michigan, my confidence rose. But I'd wait to text Pres my shots, so I wouldn't look desperate. I still had some self-respect left. Satisfied and hungry, I went downstairs.

In the sitting room, Mom held my stocking. It was red with *Garrett* in white lettering stitched across the top.

"I didn't expect you to bring those," I said.

"I thought we could hang our stockings along the staircase and all of us could put ornaments on the Christmas tree. Here." She extended the stocking toward me. "Why don't you hang yours now? I put stocking hooks on the steps." Mom pointed to the staircase off the living room.

The farmhouse had two sets of stairs. I usually took the one off the kitchen since my bedroom was near there. The upstairs was divided into two sections. The west end with my bedroom and Lauren and Shane's, and the east end where Daphne and her family would stay in the largest bedroom.

I placed my stocking toward the bottom of the steps, then I approached the artificial tree. It looked real from afar, but once I was up close, I could see the metal branches. "I'm going to miss a live tree."

"That reminds me, I bought scent stick ornaments. They should create that balsam fir aroma you enjoy. We'll put some up when we decorate the tree. I can't spend Christmas here without creating that warmth like it's *our* home." She grabbed a gold ornament.

"Where are Lauren and Shane?" I asked.

"At his parents'. Their neighbor is a doctor, so she's checking him out. I don't think it's anything serious, but it's swollen."

I hung my head. "Not a great way to start our vacation."

"It was an accident. Anyway, decorating won't take long."

"I'll pass." Granny's handmade ornaments would trigger Mom to think about the bracelet. I'd never hear the end.

"I hope your ex hasn't stolen your Christmas spirit," Mom said.

My back stiffened at her insensitivity. I headed to the kitchen to fix lunch.

"Could you wait a sec?" she asked. I stopped, tightening my body to brace for her offensive. "I can't have you moping on our vacation. It's Christmas."

Christmas... Wasn't that when we sought peace, goodwill, and empathy, instead of forcing everyone to be merry? With a stiff smile, I turned to face her. "I'll do my best to stay out of your way."

Holding a book in his hand, Dad emerged from their bedroom just off the sitting room. He looked at Mom but said nothing.

She put an ornament on the tree, not missing a beat or looking at me. "I won't have her turning us against each other."

"You did that all by yourself." I stepped into the kitchen, needing to escape the conversation; otherwise, I'd lash out. With Mom's energy and my pent-up emotions, we'd start a wildfire.

"Excuse me?" Her voice shrilled through the house.

"Nothing," I said, opening the fridge door.

"Elena." Dad's tone was firm but quiet. "Leave him be."

"I can't have him filling this house with self-pity."

I grabbed the peanut butter and jelly then slammed the fridge door shut. Why couldn't that woman cut me a break?

Dad said something, but so low, I couldn't make him out. Mom retained her raised tone, wanting me to listen. She was repeating the words she said to me a few minutes ago... my ex, Christmas spirit, on and on... I put on music from my phone to drown her out as I made my sandwich, spreading the peanut butter so thick, by the time I added the jelly and closed it, peanut butter oozed out.

"Garrett," Dad said, placing a hand on my back. I jumped, not expecting him. "Let's head to town." He spoke the words with such force, I set my sandwich down. "We'll go after you eat."

"I'm not in the mood." I didn't move.

"To eat?"

"No, to go into town. I'll probably get some work done."

He narrowed his eyes. "This isn't a request."

"All right." He rarely demanded anything these days, so I'd go along.

As I ate, Dad joined me in the booth. I could overhear Mom muttering, but nothing was coherent. So, I didn't enjoy the sandwich as a lingering fog of tension filled the house.

❆

DOWNTOWN GAYLORD RESEMBLED a quaint city in the Swiss Alps with chalet-style buildings, gabled roofs, large shutters, and steepled clock towers. A type of town I'd enjoy featuring for a photojournalism gig.

Dad parked behind a block of businesses. "Thought you'd want to take pictures of their ice tree."

As I got out, I breathed in the clean air, refreshing as a mountain stream. Instinctively, I reached out my hand, expecting to take Pres's, but stuffed them in my thermal jacket. This place incited nostalgia; I forgot myself.

Dad and I walked across the parking lot, under a roofed pavilion, and onto the snow-covered lawn of the alpine-style courthouse. It was two-toned with beige brick on the lower level with yellow stucco on the upper levels, bordered with dark brown trim. LED wreaths with red bows lined the façade. A clock tower shaped like Gandalf's hat sheltered the front walkway.

He patiently waited as I captured several pictures; I could get lost showing the town's story. That was probably why Steven Bellevue's pictures in *National Geographic* captivated me as a young kid. They turned my interest away from the parochial confines of my life to the possibilities of unique wonders. I studied his pictures of geothermal springs in Yellowstone, the leaf-cutter ants in Costa Rica, and the "flying" lemon farmers in Amalfi. My wanderlust and imagination sprung forth, but as an adult, disappointments and detours pushed that wonder to the sidelines.

"Garrett, let's move to the tree." Dad pointed to an imposing ice tree standing like a glacier fortress. It wasn't an evergreen but an ingenious marrying of man and nature.

"Impressive."

"I've seen them before." Dad pointed to the top. "It's a metal frame with a hose running water through the center."

I wanted to climb the tree with an ice pick and set a flag on its peak with "I survived" printed on it.

Approaching the tree, I slipped on a layer of ice. Dad caught my fall, but I held onto the camera hanging on my neck. I saved it but tweaked my ankle.

After waiting a moment to let the pain subside, I hobbled closer to the tree where I took selfies of Dad and me in front of it. We took another next to the 45th parallel sign. We were halfway between the equator and the north pole, yet farther from obtaining the bracelet and Pres. I was unsure what would be more difficult.

Dad tapped my shoulder, suggesting we get something sweet. Of course. We crossed the street and went into Alpine Chocolat Haus, the place where our chocolate basket came from.

This was my toy store. They had glass displays of specialty chocolate, caramel apples, and hand-churned ice cream. The aroma of fudge and other chocolate delicacies helped me to forget my troubles.

After I quit drinking in my early twenties, I stocked up on chocolates and stored them in my apartment, my backpack, and my camera bag.

Pres once called me on my sugar craving, accusing me of using sugar as a crutch. After I denied the weakness, she challenged me to abstain from sweets for a week. I tried for three days, but after I got into a tiff with a bride's father who refused to pay the remaining balance of his invoice, I bought a chocolate milkshake at a local burger joint. It tasted great after the three-day hiatus, but I admitted my failure to Pres.

She understood and never asked about my sugar cravings after that. Maybe she was afraid to admit I had an addictive personality. She never experienced me as a drunk, so up to a point, she must've assumed I was free.

I inherited the addictive personality trait from the Mason side of my family. Gramps and Uncle Earl were workaholics, more socially acceptable than alcohol, so good for them.

Although Mom wouldn't admit it, she obsessed over decorating her or her friends' homes. She'd barely eat, rest, or socialize until she finished a project. One time, she pulled an all-nighter just to decorate a new mother's nursery. It didn't matter the woman was only four months pregnant; Mom was determined to complete it in a day.

Lauren and Dad took after the Bettencourt side. They lived life in moderation, not getting too obsessed with anything. I envied that quality.

As I walked through the shop, I didn't care if I had a chocolate addiction. I might gain a few pounds and some cavities, but it sure tasted better than the other substance I'd tried.

I strolled to the assorted truffles and specialty items. Hey, they had seafoam chocolates, Pres's favorite. As I leaned my head closer, my breath partially frosted the display's glass.

"May I help you?" an employee, standing behind the counter, asked.

I looked up. "What do you recommend?"

"Everything, but our top sellers are the caramel apples, the chocolate-covered potato chips, and the caramel corn. Are you getting something for yourself or as gifts?"

"Both. I'll start with a pound of seafoam."

"Great. We also have cow patties, our special recipe, which is like seafoam but not as dense. We have it in white, dark, and milk chocolate."

Dad put a gallon tin of cherry nutcracker popcorn on the counter. "Add whatever he wants to my order," he said.

I might as well splurge and treat everyone. "I'm paying for the popcorn. And add two cow patties in milk chocolate, two chocolate-covered pretzels, one peanut butter caramel apple, a pecan apple, two traditional caramel apples, and four bags of chocolate-covered potato chips." I grabbed my wallet. This place wasn't cheap, but it was worth paying more for premium chocolate.

Armed with gold, Dad and I walked to the back and sat at a bistro table. This shop knew their patrons as a large tank of tropical fish, including a clown fish and blue tang like the one in *Finding Nemo*, sat on a large counter behind us.

I faced a wall with a flat screen TV. *Willy Wonka and the Chocolate Factory* (the 1971 version) played, one of my favs as a kid.

I took a small sip of hot chocolate, smooth and rich, hitting the spot.

"When's your next wildlife expedition?" Dad asked.

"I don't know." I'd surrender that type of vacation for a honeymoon with Pres.

"Your work is taking off. Could you block a month or at least three weeks to explore Colorado or Yellowstone?"

"Maybe once I transition in a few years." I dabbled a week here or there once a year traveling to Colorado and shooting wildlife, but I hadn't committed enough time to it once my wedding photography business grew.

"You got lost shooting the courthouse. It probably would've been hard to get you away from the ice tree had you not slipped."

"Every town has its unique story, so it'd be a shame not to pay homage." I opened the chocolate potato chips, offered Dad one, but he declined. I placed a few in my mouth. Dang. They married salty and sweet so delicately, like they should always be together. I'd have to get more bags of chips.

"I'm not trying to pressure you, but since you don't have a family to provide for yet, now's the time to transition. Just set goals and make it happen. I'm here to help."

"Thanks. Pres asked me to make a five- and ten-year plan. I've only written where I saw myself, but I haven't created a strategy. Probably a good idea, huh?"

"It wouldn't hurt. You've always accomplished what you've set your mind to."

"That remains to be seen." While I appreciated his confidence, it reminded me of what I hadn't done. Wildlife, marriage, kids.

"Nothing would make me happier than to see you pursuing what you love. If that means moving away from Tulsa, so be it. We shouldn't hold you back."

"You never have."

"Ever since I was ten," Dad said, "I wanted to work in landscaping. Something about nurturing plants and flowers was empowering."

"Wait." I held my finger up. "I never knew you considered landscaping as a career."

"That all changed once I met your mom. She wanted me to work for Gramps. And knowing how much I'd make compared to going into landscaping, I couldn't see how else to provide financially for your mom and her affluent lifestyle. So, I told myself winning her heart was more important and worked for the oil and gas company—"

"Was it a worthwhile sacrifice?" I leaned closer to him as his story drew me in. As an adult, we seemed to have lived separate lives than what I recognized from my childhood memories.

"It was, but... I struggled for many years with resentment toward your mother as I got tired of sitting in meetings." Dad looked down. Did he secretly wish he had taken the unpaved trail?

Squirming, I couldn't get comfortable since my butt hung over the sides of the round, kid-sized seat. His career desire versus Mom's expectation explained several arguments I heard in bits and pieces through my bedroom door. "That's why you two always argued?"

"Only one part, but it didn't help. So, when Gramps retired, I wanted to quit. Since Lauren left for college, I thought it'd be the ideal time to start a landscaping business."

"Why didn't you?" I inhaled more of those chips. My offense toward Mom was amplifying, and if I didn't gain perspective, I'd lose all motivation to reconcile on this trip.

"She knew it'd keep me away on nights and weekends, and knowing I'd hire you, she knew she'd be alone."

"Might've been better than having the two of you fighting." I finished the hot chocolate.

"No, it would've made it worse. She also feared the business would deplete our investment portfolio. So, I remained at the company another twenty years."

Twenty years. Could I've endured for that long? I'd invested ten years in my career, and it felt like a lifetime already. Not that I hadn't enjoyed wedding photography, but it wasn't my passion.

"Why didn't you start a landscaping company *after* you retired?"

"I didn't have the energy to launch a new business." Dad paused. Was he contemplating if he should reveal more? He sighed then continued. "And your mom wasn't keen on me working in landscaping, but preferred I'd serve on boards of other companies and non-profits."

"I know it's Mom, but have you wondered what your life would be if you had married someone else?" I winced, not really expecting to ask this question considering the implications on my life. But I needed to know from his perspective.

"No, I couldn't go there. I love her. And while I didn't know the extent of the sacrifice I'd make when we married, I got two incredible kids out of the deal. It was worth it. But—" Dad shook his head. "I don't want you to make the same mistake. You can pursue what you're the most passionate about. And the right gal will come along who'll fit with your life."

I smiled to show confidence. "I've found the right one. And you'll be happy to know I've reached out to a planner in Vegas. I want to make enough money until I can transition to wildlife. But even if I work some in Vegas, I'll still have a base here."

I didn't know how to make that arrangement happen, but I'd

tackle that problem if I were fortunate to get back together with Pres.

"Sit with Presleigh and discuss your expectations and how you two can make it work *without* abandoning your passion."

"I will." How sobering. I wasn't carrying the weight of my hopes and dreams alone, but Dad came along too.

Chapter 16

My ankle hurt the next day. So, after lunch, I lay on the bed, placing pillows underneath my leg to prop it up. I'd ice it like I did yesterday, but first I wanted to call Pres. Yet, I needed a softer sell. I texted her first to see if she'd want to connect.

The first text was of the ice tree: This is the tallest structure in Gaylord. Incredible, right? Then shots of the venue—the barn, the farmhouse with its wraparound porch, and the rolling hills—saying: Not the desert, but MI is beautiful.

Then the cow patty: I visited a chocolate shop. They make their own Seafoam. Also, I regret about not coming to Vegas with you when we started to wedding plan. Maybe connect soon?

Once I was satisfied, I got ready for Caroline's wedding, shaving my shadow and putting on my navy cable-knit sweater Pres liked in case we'd FaceTime. Before I dated her, I maintained a short beard and long curly locks touching the back of my neck. Morgan preferred that rugged look. But Pres preferred the college prep style with a clean-shaven face and short hair. Since the breakup, I let my facial hair grow.

But she didn't call.

We drove to Charlevoix about twenty-five miles away. During the ceremony, I kept staring at the photographer, wishing my cousin would've asked me to shoot it. I would've been more comfortable behind the camera where I could focus on capturing them, instead of listening to the vows.

Once the ceremony was over, I kept close to my family, not wanting to talk to anyone. What I had lost still felt raw. As we waited to be dismissed, Pres called. My heart raced with nervous excitement.

I glanced at the aisle; Caroline and Richard were headed toward us. Talk about torture letting the call go to voicemail. I quickly texted, At the wedding. I'll call soon.

K, she texted back.

After brief hugs with Caroline and Richard, our family left for the reception held at my twin uncles' lake house nearby. They lived farther south in Ann Arbor in separate homes but went in together to buy this place. They used it mostly in the summers and for Christmas. I guess their wives got along well enough, since they usually came up here at the same time.

While maintaining a second home didn't appeal to me, I'd be open to co-investing in a log cabin with Shane and Lauren if it were in Colorado or even here in Northern Michigan. So, I understood why co-owning a vacation home surrounded by nature would appeal to them.

During the short drive, I contemplated how I could convince Pres I belonged in her life. I checked my email but didn't see anything from Cheryl.

As we pulled into the vacation home, I gawked. My uncles were well off, but I didn't expect anything this trendy, like something from *Architectural Digest.* It was a cream three-story with slate stone pillars, balconies on the second and third floors, and a four-car garage. I snapped a few pictures since Pres would like this style. Personally, it was too stiff and symmetrical. I'd want some character and imperfections to show a home was well lived in.

A large red and gold sign set on an easel stood by the front door: *Welcome to Caroline and Richard's reception. Please follow the path.* An arrow pointed left to a stone walkway with lighted Christmas trees on both sides. This led us to a walk-out basement.

I entered a Christmas village. Fake snow covered the hardwood floor, artificial trees with lighted deer, elk, and moose were placed at each corner, and wooden sleighs sat near the staircase. This was the style I'd want if I had a winter wedding.

As I glanced around the room, people, conversation, and music filled the space. Everyone was having fun with their significant other. Everything from the vows, the modern home, and the couples incited my desire for Pres. Needing to talk to her, I walked down the hallway to find somewhere quiet. A bedroom door was partially open, so I stepped inside. Then I saw Uncle Erwin (the friendlier twin) straightening his tie. I turned away embarrassed since I was infringing upon his privacy.

He faced me. "Garrett, just the person I wanted to see."

"Hi," I said, taking a step back into the hall. "Sorry, I didn't realize this is your room."

"Come in."

I walked to the tall bay windows where he stood. "How are you?" I extended my hand to shake his, but he hugged me.

"Terrific. Hey, wanted to see if you'd be interested in coming to France this summer. Caroline and Richard invited me, so I thought you and I could hike and shoot wildlife in Gavarnie. It's in the Pyrenees mountains and has amazing sights with waterfalls, rivers, and unique flora and fauna. What do you say?"

"That would be incredible." I'd never been to France before.

He put his arm around my shoulder. "Look, I've got connections at *National Geographic*. Perhaps they'd want to feature your shots if you could capture enough."

My phone rang. *Pres*. "Sorry, it's my— Well, I've got to take this."

Uncle Erwin waved, giving me permission.

I left the bedroom. "Hello?" My hand shook like I was asking her out on a first date.

"How are you?" Her tone was soft.

"Good. How are you?" *Act collected, Garrett.*

"Busy with Christmas."

"Did you see the ice tree?" I walked into the bathroom and locked the door.

"Yes. It looks beautiful but cold."

"It's about twenty feet tall and at least six feet wide." I took a deep breath as my tone was higher pitched with excitement than I wanted.

"Interesting... How was Caroline's wedding?" Her voice grew distant. Did she notice my tone too? Did it turn her off? Did she call me out of boredom?

"You remembered it was her wedding." *Nah... I'm good. She cares.*

"Of course, but you probably need to visit with your family. Do you want to talk tomorrow?"

"No! I mean, now works." This was harder than I expected. I just wanted to be with her, so I came across like a boy at Christmas. "It's cocktail hour, so we're waiting on the couple to arrive."

"Hold on…. No, I will be ready in about five if you'd wait… Sorry, Garrett. What were we talking about?"

"Are you about to leave?" I couldn't mask my disappointment.

"I'm going to the church soon. I'm helping coordinate tonight's staff Christmas dinner." She was more excited than I liked.

"I'll cut to the chase," I said, talking faster than I wanted. "I assumed too much about our future. So, I've emailed Cheryl about getting on her preferred vendor list. And I plan on taking shots at the women's conferences you and your mom will host."

"You did all that for us?"

I wanted to kiss her.

"Of course. I haven't heard from Cheryl, but could you put in a good word with her?"

"Sure… But don't you want weekends off? I mean, make a fresh career here and focus on art galleries, family portraits, and sporting events or concerts. Expand beyond weddings. If that's what you'd enjoy."

"That's a thought, but how about I ease into wildlife and galleries? Weddings are for the near future, so we have money for us, a house, and kids. There's a lot to cover, but you're about to leave." Hope arose, so I could wait to finish this conversation.

"Hold on…" She sounded distant. I waited as the silence amped up the suspense, wondering if I was about to be let down again. "Sorry, I told Mom to go on. I'll meet her there."

"Thank you." What was I worried about?

"The other day," Pres said, "I walked past a photographer shooting a wedding and wanted to call you. Yesterday, I went hiking and thought about how you'd identify the various trees and wildflowers."

Was that a sniffle or a light sob?

"I wasn't sure if you'd thought about me since you've been home, but that's what I needed to hear," I said.

"Of course, I have. Look, I was hasty to call our engagement off. I just didn't want to hold you back, but since you're confident we can make it work—I know this is last minute—can you fly here on the twenty-sixth? I haven't cancelled the reception venue, but they need a thousand-dollar down payment by the end of the month. And there's a couple who want to marry at Dad's church on that same Saturday, but I asked Dad to wait."

Hasty, make it work, fly here... Those words were gifts. My angst, fears, and sadness evaporated. I was as happy now as on our engagement night. "I'll book a flight from Monday to Thursday."

"Okay... Oh, Mom didn't leave... Gar, I better go, but keep me updated about the plane tickets. It'll be a blast to hike, wedding plan, and hang out with my Vegas friends."

"I love you, Pres. Thank you."

"Love you more."

After I hung up, someone knocked on the door.

"Garrett, is that you? Are you done in the bathroom?" Uncle Earl asked.

I dropped the phone but caught it as his voice shot me back to the reception.

"Sorry, I'm done." I unlocked the door then opened it. Uncle Earl scowled in his black tux. "It's all yours," I said.

Hopefully, he wouldn't mention the bracelet or my singleness. He had a traditional view of life. You marry before or right after college, start a family, and settle into a lifelong career hopefully at one company. Any deviances, and he'd lump you into the category of adult juveniles living in their parents' basement.

"I expected you'd be mingling and drinking now that you're back on the market." He shook my hand.

"No, I just celebrated ten years of sobriety." I turned away.

"Good for you... Um... Are you interested in getting married? Or too hooked on the single life?"

"I will marry one day." I wanted to tell him Pres and I were back together, but he'd blab it to Mom.

"Don't put it off. Just because you can attract the ladies now, you turn the corner and suddenly you've put on an extra twenty pounds and have a receding hairline."

I ran my hand through my thick hair. Man, could he get to me. "I've got other things to worry about."

"You haven't lost your entitled attitude. Must be nice to work one day a week, then enjoy hiking, rock climbing, and whatever else you do in your spare time. Just to warn you, most women want a responsible man who thinks beyond the present day."

I stood tall. "Last time I checked, I completely booked my calendar for the next two years. That's how it is for a small business owner who does his own bookkeeping, marketing, and editing. But what would a millennial, who moved out of the house after college, know?"

Earl sneered. Nothing I could do would earn his respect. "I stand corrected. But I wish you had put as much care into protecting my mother's bracelet. Let's hope your ex didn't gamble the bracelet at the roulette table."

He was a piece of work!

"Pres doesn't gamble, and I'm confident we'll find it."

"Dreaming won't bring it back. I've advised your mom to be more aggressive. Press the police to investigate every suspect in the surveillance videos and hire a PI to track that Jordan character down. Because if it's not found by the next month, it's too late."

Really? He's pushing too? "We'll find it." I massaged my temples.

He buttoned the middle button of his jacket then entered the bathroom.

I joined my family at the table near the back. A pinecone held a placard with my name in red calligraphy. I struggled focusing on my family, as my thoughts were on Pres. Fortunately, everyone still expected my reticence, so they didn't attempt to coax me out of my shell.

Once the couple cut their cake, I dashed to the dessert table. I grabbed a piece of cake, a sugar cookie, and a cupcake but as I stepped away, Uncle Earl's comment about my weight echoed in my mind. In Ciaran's posts, he looked athletic. So, I returned to the table with only the slice of cake.

I sat alone, but I didn't mind the solitude. It gave me space to replay my conversation with Pres. I still needed to process we were back on, but my revelry didn't last long enough.

"Garrett!" Caroline approached and gave me a hug. "Glad you made it. How are you?"

"Good." I pulled a chair out for her.

Richard shook my hand. "Good to see you." He sat across from me.

"Same here," I agreed, although I barely knew him.

Before Caroline sat, she whispered, "I wanted you to be our photographer, but Richard wanted his brother to gain experience. I'm hoping he caught Richard crying as I walked down the aisle and other intimate moments you would've."

"It's all good," I said.

"We wanted to catch up and tell you not to worry about the bracelet. The pearl-drop earrings coordinated with my gown perfectly." Caroline pushed away strands of hair from her ear, revealing the earrings. "It was Grandpa who pushed for me to wear the bracelet." Of course, Uncle Earl would.

"Good to know." I turned toward the window. My cousin slightly resembled Granny with her lithe ballerina figure and auburn blonde hair.

"Sorry about Presleigh, but she lost out. You're quite a catch. Don't be surprised if gals slide into your DMs once the news gets out."

I smiled. "Thanks." What a relief that I had talked to Pres; otherwise, with everyone's sympathy, I would've sunken into a deeper depression.

"Did you take time off for a honeymoon?" Richard asked.

"For now," I said.

"Why don't you visit us in France?" Caroline clapped her hands. "We'd take you hiking in Gavarnie. It's the most picturesque place—it's a cirque in the Pyrenees."

"Maybe. Uncle Erwin mentioned visiting you there this summer."

"We invited your parents, along with Lauren and Shane," Caroline said.

"I'll see." Hmm... Since Pres and I were back together, that vacation would be during our honeymoon. Would Pres indulge me a few days in Gavarnie? I couldn't imagine her hiking for nine hours on our honeymoon. And I wouldn't want my family around. I'd have to see the Pyrenees another time.

"Awesome. Well, Mom's signaling us upstairs for the first dance. Love ya, cuz."

I stayed downstairs until after the groom and his mother danced then headed upstairs. But by this time, my ankle hurt again.

I sat on the sectional away from the dance floor. It resembled an ice rink, with a projector on the ceiling casting silver icicles and blue snowflakes below. Images of ice skating with Pres at Winterfest flooded my mind. I couldn't wait to see her in a few days.

Chapter 17

Once we arrived at the farmhouse, I booked a flight to Vegas for Monday. I wished I were there already, especially after hearing Pres's voice and knowing how much she missed me. I needed the next three days to fly by. I grabbed my phone to call Pres, but someone knocked on my door.

"Who is it?" I said, irritated at the intrusion.

"Lauren. We're about to watch *It's a Wonderful Life*."

"I'm headed to bed," I said with a softened tone.

"Dad's staying up."

Dad... I'd better ask if he'd give me a ride to the airport. "I've got to ask him something." I stood, walked to the door, and opened it.

"You better go now, since we're about to start the movie." She had the patience of a teenager.

I rolled my eyes. "I'll make it quick."

Downstairs, Dad was walking toward the living room. I stopped him and asked for a ride. He was cool with it, so it seemed. Then as we discussed the new plans, Mom appeared from the bedroom.

"What's going on?" she asked. "Are you hiding something?"

I turned to face her. "It's nothing that can't wait until the morning."

"No, tell me; otherwise, I won't be able to fall asleep." Mom raised her brows.

"I've got to join the kids," Dad said. "I don't want to keep them waiting."

"K..." I wished he'd stay to support me, though. I looked at Mom. "Aren't you going to watch?"

"I'm headed to bed."

"Alright..." I looked down, wishing I waited until the morning to ask Dad. I could be talking to Pres instead.

"How about we talk in my bedroom? It might be loud as they watch the movie," Mom said.

I followed her. An immaculate stack of Christmas gifts stood in the far corner, the bed neatly made, and no clothes or suitcases in sight, unlike my room.

She sat on a padded bench at the foot of the bed and then tapped the empty spot next to her. "Here, sit...". She knew something was up because she wore a fake smile with slightly exaggerated brows and squinted eyes.

"Don't freak out..." I paused as Mom's eyes grew large. "But I talked to Pres last night and..." Mom's mouth gaped. "We're going to make it work, so—"

"What does making it *work* mean?" She frowned.

"We're back together. I'm flying to Vegas on the twenty-sixth to see her." I released the words fast in our duel.

Mom jerked her head as if I inflicted a blow. She said nothing for probably half a minute. She stood and looked at the ceiling as she mumbled under her breath.

I waited for a rebuke, but she raised her arms.

I stood, placing my hands in my jeans pockets. "Say something."

She approached the back wall near a couch. She held her head high, standing above my news. "Why?" Mom turned to face me. "She admitted she'd hold you back."

"I love her."

"Is Vegas and her dad's church the life you want? If it is, I'll support you. If it isn't, then you're desperate because you don't think anyone better will come along. And in that case, I can't stand here and watch you make the biggest mistake of your life."

I opened my mouth but shut it, angry at her disrespect. I counted to ten then ripped into her. "My mistake was not demanding you apologize to her dad. Instead, it caused division between the families. So, don't talk to me about mistakes."

"I won't apologize for telling her dad the truth. You won't be happy in that church or their culture..." She took a deep inhale, winding up like a pitcher. "It'll break my heart to lose you to her."

"You never listen. I'm happy with her. End of story!" Done with our dog fight, I turned toward the door.

"I'm sorry, but if you go on Monday, I won't attend your Vegas wedding."

I paused, the air heavy and low like a fog. Wanting to release my fury but knowing it'd only further deepen the gap between us, I faced the window with the shades pulled down and trapping me inside.

"I'll attend the Tulsa reception *if* she has one," Mom said as if to satisfy any guilt she felt.

"You're not going to control me like you did with Dad and his career." As I faced her, wrath grew in my chest, ready to release the dragon within.

"That's unfair! We did what was best *for* the family...while Pres does what's best for her. So, I'm sorry, but I can't watch her take over your life." She narrowed her gaze.

Her arguments were rhythmically pounding a drum continuously, overtaking all sounds, all thoughts, and all emotions, emptying my soul of life. I cupped my ears to silence the noise.

"This is why I almost swallowed those pills," I blurted, experiencing that same numb desperation back in college. "Yet you haven't changed." The room spun, so I leaned against the wall.

"What?" Mom said, sitting on the couch. "Why are you being dramatic? Are you saying you almost killed yourself *for her?*"

"No." Wanting her to take in my anger, I bolted toward her. "It happened during the time Dad moved out. I asked if I could live with him and Lauren, but he said I had to live with you. So, I did. But you..." I pointed to her chest, my fingers just a few inches away.

"Loved on you? Fed you? Made your bed and cleaned your room?" Her face became tight like a cinched bag.

"No! Interrogating me about Dad. Demanding I spend every weeknight with you instead of at my buddy's. Expecting me to attend church every Sunday."

"What about your addiction playing a factor?"

"Yes, it did along with losing my academic scholarship and having Skye put to sleep, but my depression stemmed from family issues—especially your control." I extended my arms to emphasize my words. "I'm not blaming you, just painting a picture of how your fear of losing me played into my depression. And all I could see was our broken family and my addiction. What kind of future was that?"

Mom covered her face. "This is too much."

My mind went blank, and I didn't know what else to do except leave. As I closed the door quietly, Lauren came out of the kitchen, carrying the tin of cherry nutcracker popcorn and a tray with the caramel apples.

"We forgot the snacks." She stopped and furled her brows. "Is everything okay?"

I shook my head. "Please calm Mom down. I'm going to my room."

Mom's sobbing broke through the walls of her bedroom. I shot a glance at the door. Was she crying because I admitted my desperation as a teen, or was she hurt I was leaving for Vegas? Either way, I was frustrated how she made it about her.

"What's going on?" Lauren asked, stepping closer to me.

"I can't talk about it right now."

"K... I'll check on her."

As I went upstairs, I overheard Lauren tell Dad and Shane that everything was cool, but they should continue the movie without her. She'd be right back. Shane said, no, they'd wait.

I wanted to leave for Vegas now. I locked the bedroom door then stared out the window, wondering how Mom and I got here. The wind gathered energy as it howled, ready to burst through and throw me out into the cold. The icicles formed hardened sheets of murky film, filtering the light.

I'd never have a Christmas like this again. I'd spend it in a separate vacation rental or in Vegas.

Pres called. I dashed to the desk where I left my phone.

"Garrett, have you booked the flight?"

"Yes, I was about to call you."

"Oh no. Well, I'll pay the rebooking fee. Dad didn't think it was fair to ask you to leave your family. I'm sorry... My hands are still shaking. We got into it just now."

I hung my head, disappointed I wouldn't see her Monday and frustrated with our parents. "I got into it with my mom—"

"Was she upset you're coming here during the break?"

"It's deeper than that, babe..." I paused, not wanting to alarm her about the dynamic between Mom and me. "But she'll come around."

"We all have family conflict. Take tonight, for instance. Dad called me spoiled. Do you think I'm entitled?"

"Not at all," I assured, wanting to comfort her.

"I love you! I asked Mom, and she said I wasn't."

"Does he have another reason for delaying things, other than me leaving my family?" What if her dad was also against us marrying?

"I don't think so. He mentioned having you come after the new year."

"Good, good." I exhaled in relief. I couldn't handle both families not accepting us. After all, her dad gave me his blessing when I had asked him weeks before the proposal. He didn't give a resolute *yes*, but a soft affirmation. Come to think of it, his chest heaved as if second-guessing himself. Should I be concerned?

"So, can you fly out here New Year's Day?" Pres asked eagerly.

"Yep, I can't wait to see you. So, we're on with the reception venue and the church?" I needed that confirmation as I was wrapping my head around all the complications we faced.

"Of course. Dad will pay for the reception space by the cutoff date and tell the couple to reschedule their ceremony to a different day."

"Sounds good." I laid on the bed.

"I'll miss you, but it's only a week away... Perhaps while we wedding plan, we can decide when you'll move here." Pres was probably sitting at her desk with her Day-Timer.

We continued to talk about the wedding—well, Pres did. I listened, when after a while as I came down from my angst and relaxed for the first time tonight, someone knocked on the door.

"It's Lauren. Hold on, babe." I yelled toward the door. "I'm on the phone."

"I'll call you later. Just enjoy your family," Pres said. "I love you."

"Love you."

When I opened the door, Lauren winced. "Sorry to interrupt, but I wanted to give you the latest."

"Is she still hysterical?" I asked, still miffed at Mom's overreaction.

"She didn't mean what she said about not attending the wedding."

I sat upright on the bed. Lauren sat on the floor near my feet. "Did she say that?" I glared. I didn't want her to put words in Mom's mouth.

"Kind of... More like she doesn't want to attend now that you're cutting the vacation short and choosing her family over us."

My back stiffened. "That doesn't lessen the sting."

"I know... Why didn't you open up with me when Dad moved out of the house? I never knew you were tempted to end your life." Lauren's eyes were soft and slightly moist.

"She told you, huh?" I asked. I had only told my therapist about the pills.

"She was incredulous you'd contemplate suicide, but I think she was deflecting shame."

"I was only tempted for just a short time." I paused, recalling a painful memory. "Remember Marcie?"

Lauren nodded.

Marcie and I were close friends growing up especially since our moms were best friends. She'd help me with homework; I'd give her photography lessons. But once we reached high school, our friendship dwindled. With my parents' marriage on the rocks, I was partying hard. And she was studious and avoided parties, so I avoided her, concerned she'd pick up on my drinking. During our sophomore year, her dad died and her best friend moved to California.

One Friday night, Marcie came over with her mom. Since I was about to go out with my buddies, I barely listened to her. She ended up mumbling something about how she was wasting my time, so I left. A month later, she committed suicide, and Mom told me about the suicide note.

Something about how alone she felt, and she no longer had anything to live for.

"For the longest time," I said to Lauren, "I kept the program from the memorial in my dresser, telling myself I was honoring her. But in reality, I did it more to lessen my guilt. Since she didn't party with us, I avoided her because I was ashamed of my drinking."

"You shouldn't have blamed yourself. Marcie was always so peppy and smiling—at least whenever I'd see her. How could we've known?" Lauren shrugged.

"Maybe. I never could understand why Marcie wouldn't confide in her friends—until Mom and Dad's issues accelerated. I kept everything inside as depression overwhelmed me. I assessed that I was weak, but no guy wants to admit he can't handle life. We're working hard to prove we can adult..." I paused, fighting off my mental angst.

"Take your time, bud," Lauren said.

"Life became lonely since I was too ashamed to open up. No one explained that depression was a silent killer." I closed my eyes and took three deep breaths. "So, every time I went to write the suicide letter, I'd see Marcie's smile, telling me, *life will get better*. I wasn't convinced it would, but in faith, I eventually flushed the pills down the toilet. I was more upset I wasted my booze money." I opened my eyes to reorient myself from the memory of my college dorm room.

"Maybe this question is selfish because I want to ease my guilt, but if I had been more attentive to you during your college days, would you have shared your struggles?"

"No, I was afraid you'd go to Mom. And then she'd freak and admit me to Laureate." Relief lightened the weight as I finally shared my fears.

"But then I wasn't really in a great position to be of use, either. I was worn out from mediating between our parents, feeding Dad, and dating Shane. I don't know how any of us survived." Lauren covered her cheeks with her hands. "We need to do something differently in this family if we want healing. Once you stopped drinking, we assumed everything was 'normal', but it wasn't. What can I do to help with Mom?"

"If I knew, I'd have already taken matters into my own hands." I sat on the floor with Lauren.

Now was my chance to get something off my chest. When I was in college, my therapist advised me to tell Lauren how I felt. So, I told her that at least one of us could hope for our parents' reconciliation. I meant it as sarcasm, accusing her of turning a blind eye since I resented how she walked scot-free from pain. But back then, she smiled, as if to interpret my comment as a pat on the back. I never brought that subject up again after that.

"I need to clear the air between us," I said.

She shook her head. "Really?"

"I resented you when Mom and Dad nearly divorced. You acted so nonchalant, unbothered by their drama."

"I did struggle a lot, but I had Shane. And I kept talking with Mom and Dad. When Shane and I discovered your drinking problem, we sat them down."

"I didn't know."

"How could you? You were in the storm of addiction. Shane advised me to operate behind the scenes, while we gave you space after your intervention. Back then," Lauren continued, "you were so angry all the time and barely talking to us. I was afraid if I tried to comfort you or explain what I was doing on your behalf, you'd think I was babying you."

"I was a handful, wasn't I?"

"You didn't own the market on that. We all brought our dysfunction to the table. But what you need to know now is how I alerted them for not seeing what their separation was doing to *you*. They were so caught up in themselves, they neglected to see how you were suffering from their bickering."

I furrowed my brows. "How did Mom and Dad take your rebuke?"

"Mom bawled, trying to deflect..." Lauren paused. "Are you sure you want to hear this?"

I nodded, wanting insight on how Lauren dealt with Mom during my addiction.

"Mom blamed Dad for his passivity. You, for not coming to them about your addiction sooner. And me, for not keeping better tabs when you'd visit OU."

When I was in high school, Lauren attended University of Oklahoma. My buddy and I'd drive to "visit" our siblings on many weekends. These trips were more about getting away from my parents than hanging out with her. We'd hang out during the day, but at night, I'd party with my buddy and his older brother.

"I didn't know she blamed *you*," I said.

"I didn't let her get away with avoiding responsibility."

I shook my head. "It's not that easy between Mom and me."

"I don't care if she has twelve meltdowns, you can't continue like this. You're only enabling her."

My ankle began hurting, so I laid on the bed, propping up my leg on a pillow.

"Bud, you can do this." Lauren stood and walked toward the bed's edge.

"When she gets overly emotional, I get numb. Then I can't think of anything to say. That starts a vicious circle, where she accuses me of giving her the silent treatment."

"Tell her you need time to process, but promise once you're calm and clear-headed, you'll open up. She'll know you're not shutting her out. Sometimes your reticence comes across as punishment." Lauren gave me the half-closed, stink eye of rebuke.

I looked away. "I'm not manipulative."

"No, but when emotions are high, I'd be good to let us know you're willing to talk eventually. It's hard to know what's going on in that huge noggin." She tapped my head.

"Sometimes bigger is better." I raised my brows, too exhausted to continue the intense topic.

She rolled her eyes. "Men."

Chapter 18

Awoke up around seven in the morning desiring Pres. I'd suffered from desire in so many shapes: wanting to discover something in wildlife, capturing an image that moves people, gaining respect from peers and family. But this need to be with Pres went beyond those.

So, why was I hesitating to change my flight to New Year's Day? Something held me back. Could it be confronting the angst with her father? Would seeing him tell a clearer story than what Pres was sharing? That gnawing truth in the back of my mind I didn't want to address? Or that I didn't know how to reconcile our families?

I wasn't ready to sort through these chaotic thoughts, so I figured snowshoeing would expend energy and allow me to capture winter shots. The weather forecast indicated a storm would hit in an hour, so I had to go now.

After I put on layers of clothing, I retrieved my hiking pack, putting my camera, extra batteries, and gear in it, then headed downstairs. Small sweat beads formed on my neck and forehead.

I entered the kitchen as Mom peeled Granny Smith apples at the counter. All the ingredients lined up like soldiers behind the large mixing bowl. I wanted to linger as they reminded me of Granny, but a pause to absorb the aromas was enough to appreciate the memories.

I walked past Mom in silence, still frustrated about last night.

"Good morning," she said with a half-smile. "How did you sleep?"

"Fine." I approached the coffee station, irritated she acted congenial as though her outburst never happened.

"Sebastian called around six this morning. He wished us a Merry Christmas and asked about you," she said.

Sebastian was my parents' Italian friend. I met him in Amalfi, Italy, when I was twelve. He owned a seafood restaurant there, although I didn't appreciate the food then as I would now.

"How is he?" I asked since I liked him.

"Slowing down now that his sons have taken over the restaurant. He still goes in a few days a week, but he's hosting food tours. He's enjoying that."

"He's a people person." I poured coffee into my thermos.

"How about going to Amalfi for your honeymoon? Sebastian would recommend the best places to eat, where to stay—not that you'd have to stay there, but somewhere nearby like Sorrento. And you could see all the spots you couldn't on our trip."

I turned to face her. It'd take more than her passive apology to remove the sting of her words.

"Do you still have your pictures from that trip?" Mom asked.

"I've kept the photo album." The wind was blowing hard and echoing through the window. I needed to get outside now. "And in my office, I have the two you framed." I caressed my neck as it tightened, wondering what Steven Bellevue would think of me shooting weddings, not wildlife.

"I was proud of how you sacrificed to rescue the girl." Mom paused from peeling apples.

I rolled my eyes. "I didn't have a choice."

"But you found her and got rewarded."

"I suppose..." I poured three packets of sugar into the thermos. I regretted not taking a risk and pursuing wildlife photography. To deflect my attention from that unwelcome thought, I looked at Mom. "Anything else you want to say?"

"I'm trying to let go. It's hard when I see so much."

"No apology?" I added creamers to my coffee and stirred until the liquid mud turned beige.

"I'm sorry for hurting you. I shouldn't have blurted out my words in anger, but I'm frustrated that everything is about *them*. You having to fly to be with her. Is that how every Christmas will be?"

That wasn't the base of our fight last night; it was about her fear of losing me. But if I attacked that fortification, she'd only toss grenades. "No. We'll probably alternate Christmases between Tulsa and Vegas. And you don't have to worry about this year because I'm not flying out on the twenty-sixth, but..." I paused, still irritated by the change in plans. "I'm hanging here for the rest of the vacation."

She smiled. "I thought you bought a ticket."

"I did, but her dad stepped in. He didn't want Pres taking me away from here." Hopefully, she'd think better of Pres's dad.

"When did this happen?"

"Last night, but he didn't realize I had bought the ticket. I'll reschedule it for New Year's Day." I wore a faux smile, unhappy I'd have to wait another week before seeing Pres.

"Thank you." She nodded in satisfaction.

I tightened the thermos lid, sealing it. "Will you call and apologize to her dad about Thanksgiving?" I needed to capitalize on this opportunity while she was humbled.

Mom winced. "I suppose, but I can't call until the twenty-sixth. There's a lot of prep work here. So, promise not to nag me about it?"

"Really?" I tilted my head.

"All right... oh, I'm making apple chips too." She resumed peeling. Apple skins fell on the cutting board like ribbons.

"Perfect. The chips will be fresh out of the oven when I get back." My stomach growled. I needed breakfast, but I'd eat on the go.

"Where are you going?" she asked.

"Snowshoeing."

"We're getting three to four inches of snow, ten to fifteen mile-an-hour winds. And should you be out there with your ankle?"

"I iced it last night, so it hardly hurts. And being in the cold will be like icing it again. Two birds, one stone. Or should I say, one snowball?" I raised my brows.

"All right, comic, why don't you take some blueberry pancakes to go?" She gave a half smile.

"Will do." I was relieved she wasn't pressuring me to stay in. I walked to the dining room where I set the thermos on the table. "Where's everybody?"

"Dad and Shane are at his parents checking out his dad's new golf simulation game. Lauren's taking a shower."

"K." Perfect. Everyone was doing their own thing.

Mom handed me a large storage bag with ten steaming silver dollar pancakes and another bag of sausage. "That should be enough," she said. "I buttered the pancakes, but I didn't add syrup. And I barely heated the sausages, but they should be warm."

I placed the bags on the table next to my thermos. "Thank you."

Lauren came downstairs. "Daphne and Mike are about an hour away. He's determined to make it here before the storm gets worse."

"I can't believe they're driving in this," Mom said.

"Daphne assured they'd stop frequently if necessary." Lauren looked at me. "Where are you headed?"

I didn't want to listen to her lecture about the weather, so I grabbed my backpack quickly, then made a beeline to the front door.

"Garrett," Lauren said, hands on her hips. "I'm talking to you."

"Yes, I'm going snowshoeing." I slipped into my snow pants, jacket, and waterproof boots.

"In this weather?" Lauren's tone went sharp. "You really shouldn't."

I glanced outside the window and only could see blindingly white showers. I'd better get out now. "I'll be back in an hour." I winked then walked out to the attached garage.

After I grabbed all the snowshoeing gear, I put on my gloves as I walked into the blistering cold. My breath swirled like puffs of cigarette smoke. The snow pounded my face like pine needles. I'd hiked in bad conditions before, although it wasn't much fun.

Once in the open fields, I put on the equipment and trudged toward the alabaster hills. The wind scattered snow in all directions like confetti.

My goal was to explore the deciduous trees in the thick woods. How many times did I explain the difference between a redbud tree and crape myrtle or between a dogwood and Bradford pear, when Pres and I'd hike or drive through a beautiful area of town?

Whoo... Whoo... howled the wind, like demons echoing through a tunnel. *Creak...Creak...* moaned the trees as they swayed back and forth, as though they'd step out of the ground and walk toward me like Ents in *Lord of the Rings*. A little disturbing but mesmerizing.

Realizing this opportunity, I grabbed my gear, prepped with a telephoto lens for capturing wildlife. I opened the finger caps on the gloves, set the goggles on top of my hat, then snapped several shots of the trees until my fingers were like frozen nubs.

Suddenly, a doe stepped out of the woods about fifty yards away. I almost dropped my camera in my eagerness to capture her. She was a beauty—a whitetail with white fur around her eyes, a white diamond on her nose, and a white circle on her throat. Her long, slender legs gracefully stepped through the deep snow.

She dipped her black nose into the weedy grass popping up like a scruffy beard. I captured a few photos, but when I squatted down to shoot a different angle, I stepped on a tree branch. *Crunch.* Her long ears raised then she bolted into the woods.

Crap! I only had three pictures. I checked them quickly then snowshoed into the woods.

The wind grew stronger, so the snow fell harder. I had less visibility, but I was determined to find her.

I needed something hot to drink. Where did I put the thermos? I checked the side pocket of the pack, but I didn't see it. I unzipped the front pocket, but it was empty. Uh-oh... I left the thermos and the pancakes on the dining room table. I grabbed the hand warmers and stuffed them inside my gloves.

Although hungry and parched, I followed the doe tracks. My ankle ached, making my progress slower than I'd like, but I couldn't stop. I needed to capture the doe to prove I could move people with my art.

My GPS watch showed the temps had dropped ten degrees to 15 F. I couldn't feel my toes or fingers. How many times had I endured worse weather when capturing wildlife in the Rockies? I'd be fine.

In the wooded valley below, a doe was on her hind feet, eating leaves from a cedar tree. My heart raced. I quickly took a few steps closer to capture the frosty crystals on her fur and nose. *Bam*! I tripped on a large branch sticking above the snow, rolled down the hill, and landed on my back.

Crack! I felt a sharp object in my midsection. I reached my hand underneath my back and retrieved the object. It was a slightly dented camera body. I felt around and found the detached lens. Although this was a hobby camera, it was still expensive, so I didn't want to pay for another one.

Not wanting to suffocate, I mustered all my strength, rallying my abs, arms, and quads, as I counted to three. Then I yelled and sat up while clutching my camera body and lens.

Pricks like electrical surges ran through my ankle. I tried to free my leg out of my snowshoes, but they pulsated from inflamed muscles. The layers of snow buried my snowshoes. Everything trapped me here. My ears, nose, and cheeks, although covered in the balaclava, were hardened like stone.

Where were my pack and the poles? It'd be trickier to get up without them. I took deep breaths since I didn't want to panic and flail like a drowning swimmer. I must preserve energy if I wanted to trek back, especially before frostbite claimed my feet and fingers.

Looking around, I didn't know where I was or how someone could find me in these elements. I had snowshoed past a red house, but they'd have to travel past two hills and through the thick woods to find me.

My throat was parched from thirst and anxiety. I'd sell my camera for some scorching coffee. If only I could call Dad, but I couldn't see my backpack where my phone was. "I need help, God!" I said.

Only the screeching wind responded. Adding salt to my wounds, a blanket of snow fell from a thick branch, landed on my face, crept through my mask, and melted in a cold damp puddle on my neck. I wiped it with my glove, but that spread the water farther into my chest.

"Really?" I looked up but could only see white falling bullets.

I pushed, rested, and pushed until physically exhausted and breaking out in sweat, yet I couldn't escape. My pulse accelerated like the storm.

My body and mind detached, as if I watched myself from the naked oak above me. Everything became stiller, slower, silent. I was succumbing to the storm's power.

I was unsure how much time passed, but a faint mechanical roar echoed in the valley. *Grrr. Rrrr. Vroom.* It became louder and louder. Could it be a snowmobile? I waved my hands back and forth. "Help! In the valley!"

The engine shut off, leaving me with the howling of the wind. But then a voice calling, "Garrett!" reverberated.

"Over here!" I continued waving my free hand. "Over here in the valley!"

"Garrett!" Shane's voice echoed in the woods.

I rallied all my energy to yell louder, competing against the wind. "In the valley!"

"Stay there. I'm walking down."

Within minutes, Shane plopped down on his knees and then freed me from the snow.

"My handsome hero." I batted my frosted eyelashes.

"Your eyesight is intact." Shane tapped my arm. "Can you walk?"

"We'll see."

He gently pulled me up by my shoulders then carefully put me on the snow-covered ground. I hobbled forward on the snowshoes.

Whoa! Shooting pain erupted from my already wounded ankle. "I need to use your shoulders for leverage," I said.

He stopped as I reached out with my free hand and gripped his jacket at the shoulder. Slowly I trekked in my snowshoes alongside Shane as he maneuvered on hiking boots equipped with micro-spikes on the bottom. When we reached the top of the hill, he heave-hoed me onto the back of the snowmobile. Soon, he found my backpack and poles. After he removed the snowshoes from my boots, I held them and the poles. I asked him to place my camera body in the backpack. Then he drove us home.

When we reached the farmhouse, I patted him on the back. "Appreciate the ride, bro."

"Don't mention it." He stood and hoisted me up by the arms. I laid the snowshoes and poles on the snow.

Mom and Dad stood hand in hand on the porch.

"Garrett!" She released Dad's hand and came down the short steps. He remained on the porch.

I smiled. "I'm good."

She hugged me tight. After we pulled away, Shane laid his arms around my shoulders and helped me onto the porch.

"I'll take it from here," I said once we reached the front door.

He released his grip off my shoulders.

I took a brief step toward the door. "Son of a motherless goat!" Bullets of sharp pain ripped through my ankle.

"Watch your mouth." Mom lightly tapped the back of my head.

Geez, cut me a break. I didn't curse, even though I wanted to.

"He's quoting *Three Amigos*," Dad said.

"Oh... um... Let Shane help you." Mom pointed at my brother-in-law.

"I've got it." I hobbled behind Shane and Dad as Mom walked alongside me.

Once she shut the door, my body relaxed. The aroma of cinnamon, apples, and cloves wafted up my nose. At least my smeller worked. I sat on the wooden bench.

"So thankful Shane found you." Mom removed my boots.

"Makes two of us." I took my winter gear off slowly. My body tingled as heat penetrated my skin.

"You scared us, bro," Lauren said, scowling. "I told you to not go out there."

"He's safe," Dad said.

"Did Daphne and Mike make it?" I asked, changing the subject, irritated by Lauren's mothering.

"Yes," Shane said. "They're visiting my parents. Like you, they're worn out from the storm."

Mom squeezed my shoulder. "By the time I realized you left your thermos, you were gone for over two hours. Since Dad and Shane were still at the Maxwells', I called and had Shane look for you."

"Thanks." This was a rare time when her overly protective nature served me.

"I'll fix you fresh cocoa." She stood and walked into the kitchen.

"And that stack of pancakes, please. I'm starved."

"I'll fix the hot chocolate, Mom," Lauren said.

"Great." Mom looked at me. "I'll warm up the batch you left, heat the maple syrup, and put out the butter. How does that sound?"

"Good." Usually, I wouldn't want all this attention, but I welcomed it now.

"Did you get any photos?" Dad patted me on the back.

"Some of the swaying trees, but three of a doe. I got a shot of her dipping her nose in the snow with the woods behind her. I captured her almond eyes penetrating mine as if she knew me. Then as she bolted, I got her ballerina legs in midair. I needed more that resonated her beauty, but well... Anyway, could you check my camera? I broke the lens, but hopefully the camera body is intact. I put it in the main compartment of my backpack."

"Will do," Dad said. He grabbed the camera.

"How's your ankle?" Mom asked.

"It's a little stiff but not a big deal."

"If it swells, we'll have the Maxwells' neighbor check you out," she said.

"I'm good." I stood, barely putting weight on the right foot. Shane offered his shoulder, so I wrapped my arm around his, and he helped me to the booth.

Eight silver dollar pancakes and two rounds of hot chocolate with mini marshmallows later, I took a nap.

Chapter 19
Christmas Eve

I shut the door, propped my leg up on pillows, and lay on the bed as I Facetimed with Pres. She was gorgeous in a cream V-neck sweater, which made her green eyes pop. She showed me around her parents' home, since she had helped her mother decorate for Christmas.

They trimmed the artificial Christmas tree with cream, silver, and blue for the ornaments, with a crystal star topper. It coordinated with the decorations—crystal nativities, white garland, and white poinsettias were in abundance throughout the house, reflecting the modern style Pres preferred. I was relieved when she settled in the kitchen because the Christmas décor left me cold.

She propped the phone on something because all I could see was her upper body and face. She asked how I was. I mentioned the mishap in the woods.

"You shouldn't have been in that weather. I noticed a storm brewing there." She shot me that furrowed brow of correction.

"I love you." Her concern reaffirmed my confidence in us.

"When you come here in the new year, we'll meet with Cheryl not just about our wedding, but pitching your business. She's got clients who own art galleries. You could sell your wildlife photos in galleries and online. If you need extra cash, you can freelance at church and shoot family portraits. You could build a business servicing the congregation." Her shoulders went up and down as if kneading dough. "You'd have weekends free to shoot conferences, go hiking, or attend events."

I rubbed my forehead, struggling to listen while she talked too fast, throwing out scenarios I hadn't considered. I didn't want to be a portrait photographer. "I don't mind working weekends, but it'd be great to feature my wildlife and have time for more."

"You don't always want to shoot weddings, do you?" she asked.

"No, but until I get established there, I'll need to." I grimaced as my ankle throbbed.

Her body became still. "Are you second-guessing moving here?"

"No, it's my ankle. I need to take an aspirin."

"Why don't you do that while we talk?"

"I'll wait. I don't *want* to move." Not just because I was in pain, but I needed to focus. We continued to get backed into the same corner about our future. It was a bit unsettling.

She scowled. "You'd rather suffer then?"

I smiled, needing to convince myself. "I'm comfortable."

"What else are you doing today?" Pres said with a slight edge in her voice.

"Attending the candlelight service if the winds die down and the roads clear. Then we'll eat chili, open one gift, then watch a movie. How about you?"

"Same. We're having a potluck after the second candlelight service, but it's just for the staff. I'm helping Mom finish prepping for tomorrow night." She raised a ceramic mixing bowl toward the phone. "I'm making buckeyes for Christmas evening."

"Oh, you're talking my language." Other than chocolate, peanut butter was the next best thing. Once I stopped reveling about food, my mind became sober. "What's tomorrow night?"

"Since my brothers are spending Christmas with their in-laws this year, it'll just be me and my parents, so we thought it'd be fun to have staff over who're usually alone on Christmas night. Something low-key."

"I see..." Did they ever just enjoy Christmas with the family?

"What's that tone?" she asked.

"You celebrate differently than us. When do you celebrate with your family?"

She shrugged. "We go to my grandparents in the afternoon and celebrate with extended family."

I envisioned spending Christmas in Vegas...bombarded by family, church staff, and never having time to just take a nap or relax.

"Full disclosure," Pres continued. "Ciaran and his family are coming tomorrow night. His dad and siblings are visiting from Ireland. Are you good with that?"

I sat up then stuffed the pillow back under my leg. I didn't have any reservations, surprising myself. "Thanks for letting me know. How are they doing?"

"They're struggling celebrating another Christmas without his mom. So, Ciaran wanted to make this one special, which is why he asked them to join him in the States."

"That would be tough." I did appreciate Mom's ability to create a sense of holiday spirit just like Granny.

"Yeah, he finally explained why he ghosted me after his mom died. I needed to hear it because it helped me to appreciate what we have."

I wasn't expecting that statement. "How so?"

"After he returned home, he was overwhelmed by the stress of her death, straightening up her affairs, helping his siblings grieve, and cooking, cleaning, and caring for the family. He didn't have space for our relationship. After a few weeks of him ghosting me, I asked him to let me know if we were over." She shook her head. "The only thing he said back then was, 'Sorry. I'm not able to manage us.' When he provided this insight about him breaking up, I thought about how much I value what you and I have. Even though we called off the engagement, we still talked and worked things out. I respect you for that."

My body relaxed. "Thanks, baby. I love you." I slowly eased off the bed and walked into the attached bathroom. "I'm struggling not being with you." I grabbed an aspirin and swallowed it without water.

"I'm missing you too, babe." She blew me a kiss. "I'll call you tomorrow. Happy Christmas Eve, love."

"Bye, baby."

❉

THE WIND SLOWED to a whisper in the late afternoon, the snow stopped falling, and the roads cleared, so we made it to the candlelight service at the church the Maxwells attended. Daphne, Mike, and their daughter, Tori, were attending as well.

We pulled into the church parking lot. From the outside, the building resembled a warehouse with its square shape and white metal siding. But inside, it was cozy and warm with greeters, near the entry, handing out programs and hugs.

The sanctuary was a spacious room with a coffee station without a barista or espresso, but a few large coffee makers and mugs. This place carried the same comfort and intimacy of a spacious living room. I preferred a smaller church because it felt more like a family.

As we approached the center aisle to join Mrs. Maxwell saving the row for all of us, a display on the right wall caught my eye. But before I could investigate, Tori ran up to me and gave me a hug. Then I greeted Daphne and Mike as they approached. After a few minutes of casual conversation, I excused myself to check out the display.

On a long wood table, hand-crafted wooden figurines illustrated the life of Christ, beginning with baby Jesus lying in a manger. Mary and Joseph were hovering over him. Shepherds stood near the barn with sheep lying at their feet. In the middle, Jesus was preaching on a hill with his followers sitting on the ground. On the end, three wooden crosses stood on another hill. Jesus hung on the middle cross.

Suddenly, I envisioned him suffering. Salty sweat dripped onto his bloody, cracked lips. His body convulsed from his ripped tendons. And tears rolled down his face as the crowd hurled accusations and denials. Why haven't I experienced this tangible reality of the crucifixion before?

As if intervening in this moment of suffering, the pastor introduced himself as he stood in front of the worship team. No harsh spotlights, only Edison lights from the cross behind him and Christmas trees on the sides of the stage illuminated his face.

Jolted back to the service, I joined my family in the second row, sitting at the end next to Mom.

The worship team played "O Come, O Come, Emmanuel" softly. The congregation stood, but I remained seated as my thoughts raced about Vegas. I was overwhelmed with considering Pres's dad's church: multiple services, strobe lights, huge production team, and crowds. You couldn't escape people coming in all directions.

Tori tugged on my pant leg. I jumped. She smiled and then resumed singing. I slowly stood, trying to acclimate to the present. By the time we sang "Joy to the World," I was focused on the service.

The pastor shared a brief message then ushers handed out white tapered candles with paper protectors. The usher lit Shane's candle, starting the lighting of our shared humanity. Shane lit Lauren's, down the row until Mom lit my candle. Tori went to stand with her parents. With all lights turned off, only the flickering yellow-orange flames illuminated the room. The heat of the flame warmed my chin.

We stood in silence for a minute, then the pastor instructed us to extinguish our flames. In that moment of darkness, episodes in my life played like a newsreel. Avoiding church and prayer, convinced God abandoned me. Living in denial and accusing my family of lying during their two-hour intervention. Collapsing in a ball of anger, shame, and confusion once I admitted my addiction. Crawling on my hands and knees as I suffered from withdrawal symptoms, begging God to lift the tremors, dry mouth, and headaches.

Granny's bracelet flashed in my mind. *What was that?* I needed air.

Once outside, I stood under the church's portico, the nearly full moon radiating in the navy sky. A warm gust hit me, followed by a flash of green light blinking in the corner of my eye.

The woman in red appeared. Her gown and flowing blonde locks danced in the wind. Her face was still shrouded, but her

Mediterranean blue eyes penetrated through the golden haze. I reached out my hand, but she disappeared into the full moon.

"Garrett?"

I turned. Mom peeked her head outside. "Are you okay?"

Lowering my arm to my side, I nodded. "Of course. I'm about to come in. Don't wait on me."

She walked inside and closed the door. I stared at the black shadows of evergreens lining the property, the streetlamps in the parking lot, and twinkling stars in the clear sky.

Was this woman in red just a figment of my overly active imagination? A warning to avoid a seducing counterfeit of Pres? A sign to not give up on marrying her? This time, I wasn't as jolted.

❄

AT THE FARMHOUSE, we ate Mrs. Maxwell's chili and northern-style cornbread. Even though I chowed on two bowls, I couldn't resist Mom's lattice apple pie. She gave me a thick wedge and topped it with two generous scoops of vanilla bean ice cream.

Tori slid into the booth, sitting next to me. She held a plate containing a sliver of pie with a dollop of ice cream. "Uncle Garrett, you seem sad."

"Why would you say that?" I asked.

"You looked sad at church."

"I was thinking about Jesus."

"You can think of Jesus and be sad?" She frowned.

"Yes, Jesus collects our tears." I swallowed a large bite of pie. Ahh... Cinnamon and tart apples layered my palate.

"That's good, but I don't cry too much." Her hazel eyes grew wide. "Uncle Garrett, you'll be happier soon." She covered her mouth.

"Do you know something I don't?"

She laid her finger on her lips. "I can't tell."

"Is it a gift?" I whispered.

"Maybe." She laughed, then ate another bite of ice cream.

After I finished dessert, Daphne grabbed my plate. "Okay, you two, it's time to open one gift."

Tori followed me into the living room as the family gathered around ten gifts placed in the center of the floor.

Mike handed a present to Tori. She carefully opened it, placing the ribbon on the coffee table, and keeping the original paper intact. She opened a square box and lifted out a black stuffed animal resembling a toy poodle. She held it as she ran to her mom, hugged her tight, then kissed her dad on the top of his head.

When it was my turn, Mom handed me a long, narrow gift with a velvet red bow. What? A bracelet could fit perfectly inside. Yet, could I hope for a miracle?

"Uncle Garrett, don't you want to open your gift?" Tori said, holding her poodle.

I smiled. "Yes, do you want to help?"

"No. It's for you."

I ripped the paper off uncovering a thin white box. I lifted it open to find a piece of paper folded in half. Hmm... My gift was a typed-out riddle:

When you are sad, happy, or even mad,

you need someone with fur.

Her kisses are wet, her love unconditional.

Do you want her?

"Wait." I looked at my parents, hoping this gift was something alive. "You got me a dog?"

When I was ten, we got Skye, a rescue lab, as a puppy. We bonded, so I was her human. I taught her tricks like playing dead and posing for my camera. When I got my driver's license, I'd take her to Oxley to explore the woods and escape the tension in the house.

She was the last dog I had. Partially because I grieved her longer than I expected, not believing any dog could replace her. Then once I launched my photography business, I told myself

I didn't have time to care for a pet. With my busy schedule and Pres's allergy, I didn't see that changing soon.

Daphne handed me a color photograph of a blonde puppy with a red ribbon around its neck and a sign near its feet: *Garrett, will you have me?*

"A labradoodle?" I asked. Daphne ran a doodle rescue.

"Yes. Someone dropped her mother off, not realizing she was pregnant," she said.

"Where is she?" I looked around since I hadn't heard or seen any signs of a puppy.

"Once we get an answer, we'll let you know," Mom said as she rested her head on Dad's shoulder.

"Heck yeah," I said.

Mike left the room and within a few minutes, he returned with a crate with my golden-haired puppy inside.

"She's a five-month-old labradoodle. Vaccinated and potty-trained," Daphne said.

"Is she hypoallergenic?" If she wasn't, I didn't know how I could give her up.

"Depends on the type of coat," Daphne explained. "But overall, they shed a minimal amount of dander, and typically have a no-to-low shed coat, and low saliva content. So, most people with allergies can usually live with a labradoodle. Best practice is to keep their coat groomed regularly, like every six weeks."

"Much better than a lab," Lauren said.

"Yes," Daphne said.

"They don't allow pets here, but I asked the manager if we could bring her after the candlelight service. I assured them I'd keep her in a crate until Mom and Dad take her home tonight," Mike said.

The puppy stuck out her pink tongue as she circled the crate.

"She's the smallest and calmest of the litter. Shane thought those traits would be ideal for you," Daphne said.

"Calm's good." I approached the side of the crate and petted the puppy's floppy ear. Nothing was more therapeutic than touching a dog's wavy wool mane. I missed having a dog.

She licked my finger. She had white patches on her front paws, under her throat, and on her right eye.

"She likes you!" Tori said, as she sat on Mike's lap.

"You knew?" I asked.

"Yes. She's my friend. We play outside. She curls up to me when I read or watch TV. And she sleeps in my bed."

"That was only one time." Then Daphne looked at me. "She's crate trained and will sleep all night in there."

"I'd prefer she sleep on a doggie bed on my bedroom floor." I petted the puppy's chin.

Tori gave me a hug. "Are you happy, Uncle Garrett?"

"Very." I looked at my parents. "Your idea?"

"Shane's." Mom pointed to him.

"Thanks, bro." I gave him a fist bump.

"No one loves dogs in this family like you do," Lauren said.

"Did you get one for yourself?" I asked, wondering if this was a sympathy gift.

She shook her head. "She was the last one left in the litter, but we're not in a hurry."

I wiped away my tears. I appreciated my family. Then I stared at the puppy. A name popped in my head, in the spirit of Christmas. "What do you all think of Gabriella? Well, I'll call her Gabby."

"I like it," Tori said.

I stuck my finger through the crate to pet her, but Gabby licked it instead.

Once everyone opened a gift, Mrs. Maxwell gave me an extra key to her place. She suggested I take Gabby there now. Tori asked if she could come.

At their house, Tori explained Gabby's preference to play after using the bathroom. How she liked her soft sheep toy and tennis balls. How she fetched all the time. And how she liked to be petted behind the ears.

I lost track of time as I connected with my gift. This was a great day.

Chapter 20
Christmas

Our family practiced memorable Christmas traditions. We'd inaugurate the day with Mom's breakfast casserole and Dad's sticky buns. Then we'd open stockings and gifts.

By noon, we'd watch movies or take a nap. As I got older, I considered relaxing as necessary as fellowship and food.

We'd cap the night by celebrating with a five-course meal at Gramps and Granny's. Their home was like entering a Christmas village. Each room had a lighted Christmas tree, apple and cinnamon spice wafted in the air, and classical Christmas tunes meandered in the background.

After she died, her kids took turns hosting. As the eldest sibling, Mom held the first dinner, but I ate at the table numb with guilt, as if celebrating behind Granny's back.

We'd go to Grandma and Grandpa Bettencourt's after Christmas to celebrate with Dad's extended family.

So, this Christmas morning lacked that childlike nostalgia until the familiar scents of baked sticky buns filled the air. I texted Pres wishing her a Merry Christmas, even though it was six there.

Within a few minutes, she called. "Hi, Gar Bear. Merry Christmas."

"Hey, babe. You're up so early."

"We're headed to the homeless shelter to prep breakfast. It's tradition."

"Does your family have downtime on Christmas?" *Please say yes; otherwise, I'd have to take a week off after spending Christmas with your family.*

"On New Year's, we hunker down in a cabin in Lake Tahoe."

"For a week or two?" I'd enjoy doing that with her every other year.

"No, usually for three days, depending on what's going on with church. With the expansions, we're incorporating a staff retreat. That way, we can brainstorm and pray for the new year."

Why should I be surprised? Ever since we started dating, Pres had her foot on the gas pedal.

"Don't you want to just *be?* No timelines, sleeping in, doing nothing?"

"That's why we have three days off... Babe, can I call you later? Dad just informed me that we need to leave now. One woman who cooks is sick, so we have to help make eggs. Love you."

"Love you."

After I hung up, I went outside to think. Javelin-shaped icicles hung off the porch roof, so I took several shots with my phone. Then I laid on the carpet of snow to capture them from a different angle. As I raised the phone, footsteps echoed on the porch.

"What are you doing?" Lauren asked.

"Capturing an upward perspective of the icicles."

She remained on the porch while I got the images I wanted.

"Merry Christmas, little bro." She walked to the yard.

As I stood, Lauren extended her hand and helped me up. I moaned as my ankle hurt. Hopefully, it'd tolerate weight tomorrow when we'd hit the slopes.

"Same to you, littler sis."

Elbowing me, she issued a challenge. "I can still take you down."

I fluffed the pink ball on the top of her hat. "Sure. If that's what you want to tell yourself."

It didn't take long until she formed snowballs and pitched them toward my thighs, arms, and chest. I dodged them all and launched a counteroffensive at her legs.

I stooped toward the ground, gathered snow with my bare hands, and formed a volleyball-sized weapon. As I stood, *bam*, powdered snow hit me in the eye. Everything became bluish white. I couldn't tell if my eye watered from the impact or the melting snow.

"I'm sorry," Lauren said. "I tried to hit the top of your head. Can you see?"

"I'm working on it." I blinked several times until the sky became transparent blue.

"I'll lead you to the porch." She took my arm.

There, I cupped my hands, warming them as we sat on the steps. We enjoyed the quiet for a few minutes, until my mind became restless.

"When you dated Shane, how did you know that you were compatible?" I asked.

She exhaled like I stumped her. "It helped we got along with each other's family."

I didn't respond, hoping this wasn't a hint.

"I couldn't imagine doing life without him," she continued. "Even though it isn't easy to merge our lives at times, we make it work."

"Pres and I are focused on that now. I didn't expect us to struggle like we are."

"What's the main issue?" Lauren asked.

"She wants us to move to Vegas and help with her dad's church. Although to her credit—she's willing to travel when I transition to wildlife photography." I hoped Lauren would go along.

"Have you talked this over with a counselor, a pastor, or a mentor?"

I shook my head. "Not yet, but that'd be a good idea over New Year's. Maybe we could sit with her family or someone on the pastoral staff."

"Make sure it's with someone you trust too, bud." Her gaze was stern.

"That might have to be conducted virtually."

"Marry your best friend who's willing to do whatever it takes to make it work. Someone who'll compromise for the best plan together, not just whatever's convenient for one of you or is the least resistant path."

"We're sorting out how we can merge our lives together. It can get messy trying to make it work."

Lauren held up her hand. "Shane and I have worked out differences through mentors, pastors, and counselors. It's not a one and done, but a journey." She paused. "We're seeing a counselor about our infertility issues."

I winced. Unfortunately, Lauren inherited Mom's pregnancy challenges. She suffered a few miscarriages before having Lauren and one before having me. I hated that Lauren was suffering this now. "Is the counseling helping?"

"Yeah, especially teaching us to represent ourselves and accept that one of us might have a good day while the other's struggling." She frowned. "Although running into Uncle Earl at the wedding nearly stole my holiday cheer."

"Oh, he said something about your infertility?" I jerked my head. I could handle his attacks on me, but he better not have come after my sister.

"He asked when we're starting a family, even though Mom's told him about our struggle. I wanted to tell him off so bad, but Shane led me away."

"At least our uncle is an equal opportunity jerk."

"Good news. They're not coming over tonight. With Caroline and Richard leaving for France soon, they're all staying at the lake house to celebrate."

"Can't say I'm disappointed." I shrugged.

"I'm headed inside." Lauren stood. "A piping hot pecan roll is calling my name."

I'll be in a moment." I pointed at her as she headed to the door. "Don't take my middle."

"No promises." She winked.

Chapter 21

I approached the twenty-sixth as a reset. I'd usually take a half a day off unless it landed on a Saturday. I'd spend the morning assessing the past year and resolving to drop a bad habit. I'd usually sputter out after about six months, reverting to the old habit again. But the times I endured, I found freedom.

Today, I woke up earlier than I had been in Michigan, bummed I wasn't going to be with Pres today and miffed her dad put the brakes on that plan.

Even though it was only six, I wouldn't be able to go back to bed with this tension rolling through my body. The moon seeped through the small arched window, illuminating my journal on the desk.

Fine. I might as well do the inevitable. When I sat at the desk, I tapped the end of the pen on the journal. What should I quit? Hmm... I wrote, *Stop eating cruciferous greens and eat more chocolate bars.*

Are you going to take this seriously? Where did that thought come from? Sounded like Mom.

Let's see here... How about: *Stop leaving dirty clothes on the bathroom floor.*

Nope.

Yikes... Now, that really sounded like her.

I crossed off both ideas and then set my pen down. If I wanted to grow, I needed something challenging. But what? *Tap, tap, tap....* I hit the pen's end on the desk as my mind went blank.

When I turned to face the window, I knew. I turned to a fresh page in the journal and wrote my goal for 2017: *Quit Avoiding Pain.* Could I maintain this for a year? I slammed the journal closed then hopped onto the window seat.

During my addiction recovery, I worked hard to face wounds, offenses, and triggers. But after ten years of sobriety, gravity settled, and I slipped back into the habitual patterns of avoidance.

First order of business... I stared at the barn's cross. "Hey, God. How are you? Good? Yeah, as you know, I'm in a tight bind. I want Pres, but we're struggling to unite our visions. Help."

How could we make it work? No, the real question was: How could *I* make it work? In Michigan, I've relished the beauty of nature, the wide-open spaces, and the intimacy of a small community. Tulsa retained a family vibe within a metropolis, but I couldn't say that of Vegas.

After sitting in silence for about an hour, I got dressed then went downstairs.

"What are you doing?" Mom asked, standing in the kitchen. Despite the early morning, she was dressed in blue yoga pants, a lemon-yellow sweater, and an impressionist blue scarf around her neck.

"I'm going to sit outside and catch the sunrise."

"May I join you?" She set a spatula near the fruit skins on a cutting board. Yes! She was making wassail. That put me in a better mood.

"Sure," I said. At least, Mom and I appreciated food and continuing traditions.

"I'll be out with coffee for us in a moment," she said.

"Thanks. I could use a strong cup."

Once outside, I watched the sapphire blue sky blanket the farm as the full moon hung high, its glow casting orangish-yellow shadows upon the snow. Nothing better than catching blue hour with its solitary beauty. *Twerp, twerp, twerp...* Some northern bird bellowed a sorrowful melody. The soft air breathed cool whispers into my face.

Looking at the barn, the white lights along the roofline illuminated the wooden cross on the snow drifts.

Mom, in a cream puffer jacket, joined me on the porch. She placed our coffees on a small table and then sat on the twin chair.

"It's beautiful," she said. "Times like these, I miss Granny."

I nodded. "She'd be identifying the birds from their songs: That's a whip-poor-will, a sparrow, and a dove."

"A few months before she passed, she told me that I needed to listen and not minimize your experience. As a feeler, you perceive depths of emotions beyond the average individual."

"I probably wore her out sharing through the years." If Granny were here, I would've sorted out all these conflicts I had about Pres.

"She knew how much you valued her."

"It didn't matter if I was meeting with a client, she expected me to answer her calls. One time, during a bridal session, she called three times and texted five. I finally excused myself, and she asked meekly, *why aren't you here?* I felt bad about making double appointments."

"Oh, she told me." Mom took a long sip of coffee and then cleared her throat. "Uncle Earl is pushing me to hire a PI, especially because you saw the bracelet."

I got a pit in my stomach. "Can we not bring up the bracelet until we return home?"

"I knew how this would be. You and Dad will move on while I'm left tracking it. So, I'm going to hire the PI."

I formed a fist; the sky remained a sapphire blue. Why couldn't she just entrust me to track it my way? "I've been doing my due diligence, but I prefer enjoying Michigan for the remaining days."

"The PI will track Jordan. And the sooner the better because who knows what they plan to do."

"What?" I extended my arms. "You're going to sue, bully, or threaten to call the police? And what if they don't have the bracelet?"

"Too much evidence points to him. The pawnbroker talked to a Jordan. The man gifting the vintage bracelet is a Jordan. And you glimpsed it on his girlfriend's wrist... What's that scowl?" Mom put her hands on her hips. "The PI could ruffle the pawnbroker's feathers to get the truth."

I rolled my eyes. "That only works on TV."

"We'll see."

"I know we'll find the heirloom," I said softly.

Mom shook her head. "How?"

"I had a vision of a woman in red the night of the engagement and on Christmas Eve, when you checked on me in the parking lot during the service."

"That explains your distant look. But what does that vision have to do with the bracelet?"

"This woman wore it both times."

Mom touched her chest. "Was it Granny?"

"No..." I looked down, hoping she wouldn't interrogate me further.

"Presleigh?"

"Symbolically, yes. I couldn't see the woman's face."

Mom narrowed her eyes into a lioness gaze. "What do you think it means?"

"A sign from God the bracelet will return?" I wasn't about to tell Mom that I wondered if my subconscious produced the vision.

"We need to act, not rely on a vision. Otherwise, it sounds like an excuse to quit searching."

"That's not what I meant. We need to trust God it'll return to us." I took a sip of coffee, hoping she'd agree.

"And what did you mean by red? Was she a redhead?"

Why did I tell her about the vision? "She wore a red gown."

"What was her hair color?"

"Angelic blonde, but it's symbolic." I rattled off that answer to convince myself, because I didn't know who she was or why she appeared twice.

Mom leaned toward me, her blue irises penetrating mine. "Do you believe that?"

"Yes. The Bible speaks in metaphors." I looked up to avoid her scrutiny. I wasn't a good poker player.

"There's an edge to your tone. You're not sure it's Presleigh, are you?"

"What?" I stood, wanting to leave. "That's absurd."

The wind howled.

"No, it's not. She's a brunette. And even more implicating, she didn't want to wear the bracelet. If she cherished it, she wouldn't have carelessly lost it at the airport." Mom leaned back on the chair.

I forced myself to not sound condescending, but she was ignorant or acting like she was. "It could be God encouraging me I'll marry her despite the obstacles."

"If that's what you want to believe." She stood, grabbed her mug, and walked inside.

I stayed. The bluish-black night sky became grey, orange, then yellow as the sun ascended slowly. The dawn illuminated the hardened ice on the porch's railing.

Shouldn't it be Pres? Whenever I was around her or talking with her on the phone, that familiar bond assured me we were right for each other. But up north, especially during moments of solitude, I addressed questions I had ignored.

Shane came outside, standing by the door. "Hey, do you want to go tubing?"

"That might be fun." I shrugged, frustrated I couldn't go skiing. I had looked forward to it.

"Your dad wants to try it too."

"Are you coming?" I asked, hoping he'd join us. "You know, with your wrist."

"Nah. I'm going snowboarding." Shane rotated his wrist without grimacing. "It's better." He walked to the railing, standing only a few feet away from me. "Are you sure everything's fine?"

"There's a lot going on," I said.

"Like what?"

If there was someone other than Dad I could open up to, it'd be Shane. He knew how to ask questions to get me to think, not tell me what to think.

"I'm assessing if Pres and I can make it work. I haven't gotten our talk out of my head." I glanced at the Clubhouse. So much had happened since Shane and I played basketball. "Could she enjoy the month-long wildlife excursions? Could I keep up with her family's expanding ministry? For starters."

"Hum." He paused as if to weigh his words. "I wondered about the wildlife trips. You spend ten to twelve hours tracking, shooting, and editing. But I suppose she could explore the city or nearby town and meet up for dinner and read a book while you edited all night."

"I'd adjust my schedule, but I don't know if she'd leave her father's church if I got an opportunity for a three-month stint to shoot wildlife."

"Haven't you talked this over with her?"

I cleared my throat. "When I painted the picture of my career as a wildlife photographer, she deflected and offered suggestions about pursuing this or that in Vegas. I don't know if she's not accepting this option for us or assumes wildlife would only be a hobby."

He crossed his arms across his chest. "Dude, don't dance around issues. Confront her directly. Make sure she understands this career is what *you* want."

"I will." *Thud!* Some icicles fell off the roof, landed on the snow, and broke in several pieces.

"If she loves you, she'll pull her weight to make the relationship work."

"Did you want to live up here near your parents?" I gripped my stomach as it churned.

He nodded. "Lauren and I talked about this option the other day. My parents know some business owners who'd hire my production company and Lauren's design services. We might come up north for a month or two."

"Lauren seems to like it here," I said, slightly excited.

"And it helps she gets along with my folks."

"For sure." I raised my brows.

Shane smirked. "Gotta pressss her to…"

"Leeaveee and cleeaveee," I added.

"I Garr-un-tee she knows it's Biblical."

I smiled. "It'd be best for her to come to the Better…court."

"Good one, bro."

"Glad we could get this settled."

Chapter 22

When Dad and I returned from the outing, the house was quiet as the family were still skiing. We sat in the living room, looking at the photos we took of our tubing experience.

"This is hilarious." I pointed to the shot of him laughing. A few seconds earlier, he fell off the tube and faceplanted in the snow.

"You were a kid today," he said. "It's been a while since I've seen you *that* carefree."

"I didn't expect to have that much fun. Thanks for coming with me."

I laughed watching a video Dad took of me whooping and hollering on the tube. Once I reached the bottom of the hill, I slid off and raised my arms. A warrior conquering the day. All my cares melted under the winter sun.

After going through the photos, we ate pecan buns, drank wassail, and listened to soft jazz, neither of us saying anything for a while.

Dad looked at his watch and then broke the silence. "I woke up early this morning and prayed about the bracelet. And I'm discerning that God's leading us to trust him and to stop pursuing it. I shared my impression this morning with your mom after she talked to you." He smiled. "We're not hiring a PI."

"Oh..." I set my wassail on the side table. "Is she mad at you?"

"I'm giving her space. Hopefully, she'll realize it's not worth the trouble."

Trouble. I looked away. That's what I brought to the family by pushing Pres to wear the bracelet for the wedding.

Dad continued. "I told Mom the bracelet is only a piece of jewelry. While it represents Granny, it's keeping us stuck."

"How so?" I clutched my cross necklace.

"By continually calling pawnshops, the police, and whomever, we're not moving forward. It's caused a lot of turmoil between the two of you. Granny would've asked us to stop searching."

I hung my head. "Yes, she would've."

"Mom mentioned your vision of the woman in red."

"It was probably a figment of my imagination," I said.

"I find that difficult to believe. You've always been more spiritually intuitive than the rest of us."

"Not anymore," I mumbled. "Alcohol impaired my sensitivity." What else had I lost through my addiction?

"But God's restoring it... Can you trust that he gave you this vision?"

"I want to." The woman in red represented what I had lost and might still lose. I knew God wouldn't taunt me with something good, only to take it back.

Dad placed his hands behind his head. "Maybe he gave you the vision, so you'd trust him to return the bracelet."

"That's why I saw Jordan's girlfriend wearing it. How else could I explain the coincidence at The Mayo that day? I'm sure he'll put them back in my path," I said to convince myself.

"This might be difficult to swallow, but he'll return it to you in his unique way, where you won't have to pursue it or ask for it back."

I fidgeted on the couch. "I respectfully disagree. If I see it, I'll get it back."

"How did that work out for you?" Dad's stern tone frustrated me.

"I was caught off guard, but next time, I won't be. I'll show them the serial number and demand they return it to me."

"For Granny's legacy, let it go and let God work behind the scenes. If you interfere, you might delay its delivery." Dad unlocked his hands and then he leaned toward me.

Jordan's shove was fresh in my mind. I couldn't let that loser win. "I'm getting what's mine. Sorry."

He took a deep breath. "Changing the subject... Since you've been here, have you given any more thought about pursuing wildlife photography?"

I sat straighter. I didn't have a clear answer.

He smiled. "You've taken some great shots."

"Thanks. I've been inspired here."

"I want you to dream again."

I couldn't tell him I became disillusioned and quit dreaming in high school as their marriage crumbled. Reality slapped me out of my utopia of believing we had an ideal Christian family. So, as they were coming apart, I attacked other beliefs, afraid I'd be misled. I stopped having visions for a long time and started doubting I could make it as a photojournalist.

"Being here, I've experienced an awakening of my former dreams." I glanced at the wall clock with the second hand ticking continuously. "But I need another lifetime to see it through."

"Take small steps and discuss it with Presleigh. You two can make it work."

"I don't know. I'm afraid if I move to Vegas, it'd take a few years to rebuild a decent photography business. Even if I could take time off and shoot wildlife in Colorado or Yellowstone, it'd be a hobby for at least ten years, especially once we have kids." My pulse raced, knowing the energy required to rebuild my business.

"Often, you have to make the best worst choice and live with the results. And that's what you've always done." Dad smiled.

I hadn't seen it that way till now. Working for the photographer paid for school. Electing not to take Mom's handout but mailing it back. Enduring counseling and group therapy while working and attending classes. Refusing to relapse even though I nearly did multiple times. Wanting a meaningful relationship, instead of maintaining shallow ones. Each of these choices made me resilient and led me here.

I stood. "I've got to do something."

When I was in my bedroom, I stared at my phone. If Pres answered, I'd call off our engagement. If I got her voicemail, I'd stay.

She answered on the fifth ring. My pulse heightened as I gripped the phone. "Oh hi, Gar. Just got off the phone with Cheryl. What if we have gourmet chocolate favors? We'll schedule a tasting with the chocolatier."

"That sounds amazing." Nope, we were compatible.

"Oh baby, I haven't asked about you," she said. "What did you do today?"

"Dad and I went tubing." The freedom I experienced on that snow hill was what I needed. I couldn't see myself tapping that inner child in Vegas.

"I wish I could've been there. We would've had fun."

"I know." I closed my eyes. Was I about to make a grave mistake?

Boom! Chhhr... Rrrr... A mechanical roar erupted in the background, disrupting my focus.

"You sound off. What's wrong?" Pres asked.

"What's all that noise coming from?"

"It's the bulldozers and jackhammers. They're building an upscale neighborhood behind my parents' home."

"No more mountain view?"

"New builds will partially impede the mountains. Hold on, I'll go inside where it's quieter."

Shortly, the pitter-patter of her footsteps replaced the clanging of the bulldozers.

"Is that better?" she asked.

"Thanks." My heart beating was louder than the construction noise. "If we were to buy a home there, could we live in the country with a few acres?"

"It'd cost at least a million dollars and would be too far from church. Henderson's the ideal community—close to the city yet in the suburbs. There's even a climb gym nearby." Her tone became melodic, like a real-estate agent's jingle as they're selling property. "Speaking of which," she continued, not waiting for me to answer. "We should meet with the real-estate agent. She works with the developer, and we could check out the models. Or we could look into a new build. We'd have a mountain view for a few years."

The walls were closing in. I didn't want this... *Give me strength, Lord.* My knuckles were white from gripping the phone like a vise. "Could you pause for a sec?" I asked.

"Sorry, I'm probably jumping the gun. But it'll be amazing. They have a community pool with a lifeguard on duty. They plan to participate in a swim league, so it'd be ideal for our kids. And they have tennis courts and a ten-mile running and biking—"

"Babe, let me talk," I said before I'd lose my resolve. The more she talked, the more convincing she sounded especially when she mentioned "our kids".

"You don't have to be so gruff."

"I'm sorry." I looked at the cross necklace and saw my reflection. "I've given a lot of thought to us... And I don't know how better to say this, but you were right." I paused as the words I needed to say next were lodged in my windpipe. I cleared my throat and spewed out the words before I could second-guess myself. "We're not compatible, and I'd hold you back. I've enjoyed the solitude here and want to experience more. Maybe, in a year or two—"

"Slow down, babe. You're talking so fast, I can't understand you."

I didn't know where to start. So, I just continued where I left off. "I'll move to the woods on the outskirts of town. Ease into wildlife photography—"

"I'm confused. Are you saying that no matter what, you want to buy a home in the woods too?"

"No." This sensation traveled through me, detaching me from my body. I was an observer, sitting on the roof, peering into the bedroom while a version of "Garrett" talked on the phone. "I'm explaining how we're incompatible. I don't want to live in a carnivore neighborhood where they devour land for lunch. I prefer a smaller church where you know all the members. But this isn't the life you want."

Silence filled the space. No sobs, just her releasing breaths of air, like a weary swimmer struggling in the water. I waited, still detached. I refused to rescue her; otherwise, we'd drown together.

"No," she said with a sudden strength. "We already discussed how we could merge our lives. You have a great base here to fly to Colorado, Yellowstone, and even overseas. I don't expect you to work at the church. If you need the woods, one day, we can buy a house in Lake Tahoe. We'd get away there, and when we weren't using it, we'd rent it out."

I returned to my 'body' as her tentacled words wrapped themselves around me. "Maybe..." I glanced outside, the snow fell quietly. "Would you live in Tulsa for the next year and a half? I'm booked until mid-2018."

"I assumed you'd sell your business to Phil and move here."

Did she consider my career expendable? I'd invested too many hours building my business marketing to high-end couples. "These brides signed with me to shoot their weddings."

"Let me figure this out..." Rustling from papers filled the space. She was probably checking her Day-Timer. "Until we're married, I'll fly there on Sunday afternoons and stay until Wednesday. Once we're married, you could fly to Tulsa on Thursdays and return on Sundays. It'll be only for a year. When you can travel for wildlife, I'd go with you."

She was tossing me into a mixing bowl, stirring me around, adding other ingredients, and voilà—Garrett and Pres brownies.

"Listen to me," I said gruffly to drown out her voice. "You haven't addressed how I prefer a smaller congregation."

"You said it's about us making our lives work together. I don't understand why you're going against your word." She talked so fast, it took me a moment to process. Once I did, I saw in my mind's eye pliers cutting her cuffs free.

"I love you enough to do what's best for *you*," I whispered. My hands shook.

"It's about Ciaran," she growled. "Admit it. You're jealous and breaking it off to protect yourself. Afraid I'll pull a Morgan and date him behind your back?"

Whoa. I stepped back and ran into the edge of the bed.

"I hit a nerve, didn't I?" She yelled like a taunting opponent.

My body tightened like a cinched rope. "Give me a sec to process..."

"I don't understand. I felt like I had made a mistake calling off our engagement. This isn't happening." She sobbed.

Why did she have to cry? I held my hands on my forehead. I couldn't say anything for a few minutes as she mumbled under her breath. What a fool she was for paying the reception deposit. Why didn't she recognize the signs when she couldn't find a wedding gown. How she didn't want to wear the bracelet.

Why did she mention the heirloom? I pursed my lips to prevent a rant.

"Say something." Her voice screeched like car tires.

"I can't... It'll hurt you." My lips quivered.

"I'm not staying on the line. I'll leave you with this thought. You stuck a knife in my back, reneging on your promises." *Click*.

I recoiled; her words were too harsh. I collapsed on the bed. The pain was worse than when she called off our engagement. Back then, I was shocked; now I was sober. What hurt the most... I might've lost my only chance for love.

Chapter 23

Later that night, I couldn't sleep. I tiptoed downstairs to pray. The house was still. I started a fire in the gas fireplace and sat on the stone landing. The flames spat and rose behind me, warming my back. The white lights on the Christmas tree and the yellowish-orange flames provided an ambient glow. The quiet at midnight was a holy hush, calming my restless mind.

I held a pad of lined paper on my lap and a black pen in my right hand. I waited in solitude until my mind cleared.

During recovery, I wrote letters to people I hurt or who hurt me. The exercise was cathartic, releasing my angst, guilt, and shame.

When I'd revisit the letters a few days later, my accusations and anger shocked me. I blamed so many people for my choices, refusing to take ownership of my decisions. Only a few times did I acknowledge my culpability, so I mailed those. But I burned the ones filled with vitriol.

Now as I wrote, I paused several times when I got consumed with hurt and anger. Wanting to evade bitterness, I turned to the fire, enjoying the dancing flames and the tender crackling of embers.

I finished by one. I tiptoed upstairs, laid the letter on the desk, and slipped into bed.

The next morning, someone knocked on my door three times, waking me. "Uncle Garrett, we're leaving," Tori said.

I sprung out of deep sleep.

"Please wake up. We're leaving," she continued.

"I'll be down shortly." I stretched my arms and yawned.

Downstairs, Daphne, Mike, and Tori pulled their wheeled suitcases to the front door. Before they'd return home, they were visiting Daphne's grandma in town and participating in a legacy video Shane was shooting at her place.

Tori gave me a hug and asked me to watch over Gabby. I enjoyed spending time with her and getting in practice for when I'd be an uncle.

After they left, I turned to Mom sitting in the booth. "Did Shane and Lauren leave already?"

"Yes. He wanted to set up."

"Where's Dad?" I looked around.

"He woke up with aching joints, so he's checking the weather."

I pulled up the forecast on my phone. Tomorrow promised winter weather advisories with a blizzard hitting the area around nine in the morning.

We needed to adjust our schedules. My parents switched their flight to tonight. I left a message with Lauren, asking her to call.

As I helped my parent's pack, Mom frowned. "You look tired."

"I was up late last night writing Presleigh a letter."

"Oh?" Her brows furled.

"I called off our engagement. No turning back." I swallowed the lump in my throat.

Mom pursed her lips and her eyes widened. I appreciated her attempt to keep her emotions in check.

"Do you want to read the letter?" I asked, extending an olive branch.

"Sure..." She paused as if my question triggered a memory. "We've kept *your* letter."

I winced, recalling the venom I unleashed especially toward her. "You didn't burn it?"

"It hurt reading it the first time. But after I reread it a few days later, I appreciated your honesty."

"I'll fetch Pres's letter," I said.

When I returned to the sitting room, I plopped on the love seat adjacent to the couch where Mom sat. Then I read the letter out loud.

Dear Presleigh,

Hope life is good in Vegas. As I write this letter, snow covers the ground, and a fireplace warms my back. I can't complain. I've learned a lot in the last eight months. Because of you, I watch romantic comedies. I arrive to places on time (okay, that's still a work in progress), and I try to go out more. You made me a better man. You were a safe person, showing me I can trust—what I thought I had lost with Morgan. And because of us, I realized I can maintain a healthier relationship.

But I have regrets. I wish I would've faced issues before we got engaged. How I didn't fit in with your dad's church. How we had different expectations for marriage. And how our families didn't gel. And the bracelet. I know it held little meaning for you. I'm angry you were callous and careless. But in hindsight, I shouldn't have pushed you to take it to Vegas. Now, I'm trusting God to return it.

One day, you'll realize I did you a favor by setting you free. I'll always have a place in my heart for you and the times we had.

Best in life,

Garrett

Mom kissed my cheek. "I'm proud of you. Knowing how clearly you see things helps me to forgive her."

I folded the letter and placed it in my shirt's breast pocket. "Does it sound bitter?"

"No..." Mom paused. "I called her dad yesterday and apologized. I should've done that when you first asked, but I was afraid and angry that Pres and her family would take you away from us." Her voice cracked, so she cleared her throat. "Sorry. I didn't give you the benefit of the doubt."

"I needed to hear that." I flashed a wide smile. "And I'll remind you when you don't."

"Oh, I know."

I was unsure how long she'd let me adult, but I wanted to enjoy it for now.

The doorbell rang. Dad emerged from the bedroom, glanced at us, smiled, and went to the front door.

I grabbed Mom's luggage from the bedroom.

The Kayes, the owners of the venue, entered. We met them yesterday when they stopped by to check on us. Once they discovered my parents were flying out of Traverse City early, they offered to take them to the airport since they were headed there for a getaway. How convenient for me.

"Hi, Garrett." Mrs. Kaye shook my hand. With her melodic voice, I imagined sitting on their covered deck, observing whitetail deer, and eating homemade chocolate chip cookies. Their house was the red, modern farmhouse beyond the venue.

"Thanks again for taking my parents," I said.

"Glad it worked out," Mr. Kaye said, standing next to his wife. Yesterday, when he shared vignettes from this farm, he reminded me of Grandpa B—energetic, engaging, and entertaining.

"We'll keep you updated on our flights." Mom hugged me.

"Good," I said.

"Love you. Keep us in the loop about when you're leaving." Dad patted my arm.

"Will do."

"Let us know if you leave tonight, Garrett," Mrs. Kaye said.

"Do we have your number?" I asked.

"Here." She grabbed a small notepad out of her purse. After writing it out, she handed it to me.

"Thanks." I put her number in my phone.

Once my parents and the Kayes left, I headed to the Maxwells' house to visit Gabby. I stayed about an hour then returned to the farmhouse. There, the Maxwells, Shane, Lauren, and I gathered at the TV watching local news in the sitting room like on election night. The meteorologist described the storm as an arctic outbreak—wind gusts at thirty to forty miles an hour with low to no visibility.

We conferred, deciding we needed to leave tonight, so I could shoot a rehearsal dinner on Friday. Two hours later, we were ready to go. While Shane and I were in the garage putting our suitcases into the vehicle, Lauren popped her head from the door. "Marlene called. Gabby's throwing up."

"What?" I asked. "She was good a few hours ago."

"Marlene thinks Tori fed her cookies when they came over to get her stuffed animal."

My heart raced. "Not chocolate chip I hope." Chocolate could kill a puppy.

Lauren shook her head. "No, Marlene only made snickerdoodles."

I placed my hand on my heart. "Thank God. What do you want to do?"

"How about we wait for her to get better? It might take a few hours. Then we'll leave," Lauren said.

"Since we're worn out from not getting much sleep last night, I'd prefer to rest and leave early like three in the morning. The weather forecast said something about not hitting this part of Michigan until around nine tomorrow. We could be in Chicago by then. Spend the night there if it gets bad then drive to Tulsa on Thursday," Shane said.

"What do you think, Gar?" Lauren asked.

"That's probably better than driving with a sick puppy."

So, after condensing only what we needed for the night into our backpacks, we made hot chocolate. Shane filled their SUV with gas. By nine, we crawled into bed. But worried about Gabby and the storm, I couldn't fall asleep right away.

❄

THE LAST TIME I experienced a fire drill was in grade school. This morning, I experienced that same panic. My phone rang over and over, waking me up. I got up, realizing the sound wasn't a dream, then hurried to the phone charging on the desk.

"Hellooo," I said, trying to wake up.

"Garrett, it's Marlene. You haven't forgotten about Gabby, have you?"

"What time is it?" I rubbed my sleep-encrusted eyes.

"Five."

"Crap! I must've not set an alarm. And Shane and Lauren—"

"I've tried to call them, but it goes straight to voicemail," Marlene interjected.

"I see. Well, we'll be there to pick her up within the hour. How is she?"

"She had a rough night, but she's better this morning."

"Good. Appreciate the wake-up call."

I glanced outside. The moon cut through the stark darkness as the wind screamed at the panes. I walked across the hall as I put my shirt on. I knocked on Lauren and Shane's bedroom door, waking them up.

About an hour later, we picked up Gabby at the Maxwell's. Shane drove first. Lauren sat in the front passenger seat, and I was in the back with Gabby on my lap.

Unfortunately, the storm arrived earlier than expected. Snow fell heavily, like spiked darts slamming the windshield. The violent wind gusts made everything loud as we drove only forty-five miles per hour.

Driving through a blizzard was like tiptoeing through a haunted house. I didn't know what could jump out at us—a sliding car, deer, or debris. After a few hours, I was a wrung rag.

When we stopped for gas, Shane and I exchanged places. Needing to sleep, Shane put Gabby in the carrier. I drove to Grand Rapids in six hours but in normal conditions, it would've only taken three.

"The only way you'll get to Tulsa on time is to fly," Lauren said.

"I'm not leaving you hanging." I pulled into a cafe. "The weather will improve farther south."

"We're still not taking any chances." Lauren narrowed her gaze.

Shane popped up. "I agree."

"We can if we drive together. I'll drive all night," I said.

"We're not debating this," Lauren said. "Let's find you a hotel near the airport."

Although Shane looked rested, he'd be driving most of the way. "No, I'd rather see how far we get," I said.

"I'm booking your flight online." Lauren raised her phone.

"Lauren and I will stop in Fort Wayne tonight then see how far we get tomorrow. You can't risk missing the rehearsal."

This weekend's wedding was a high-end, three-day affair. They were paying me and my second shooter to document all three days. I was outnumbered. "I'll use my flight credit."

"There you go," Lauren said.

If the fifth motel we checked hadn't had a vacancy, I would've slept at the airport. Before I got out of the SUV, I petted Gabby, wishing she could travel with me. She whimpered, so I left my flannel shirt for her to sleep on.

Fortunately, I arrived in Tulsa the next day on the 29th. The storm had stopped by then, so flights could take off. I was a little roughed up as I suffered from little sleep, stress, and sore muscles, especially from the cramped plane. But what an adventure I had up north.

Chapter 24

I sat on my deck, sipping coffee and writing in my journal. I usually prayed and enjoyed the quiet morning before the hectic pace of shooting a wedding. Edison lights across the deck ceiling provided an amber glow like a campfire.

As 2016 ended, I had no regrets, especially my time with Presleigh. She served as a catalyst for writing my five- and ten-year plan, pursuing what was in my heart, and valuing my voice. We had a great ride, and I truly hoped for the best for her.

I didn't understand why, but I pictured Gramps sitting next to me sipping on root beer and telling jokes to get me to laugh. I always did. He could make a stern Russian double over.

One time, after laughing so hard my sides hurt, I glanced at him. He covered his eyes with his hands. Curious, especially since I was in the early stages of sobriety, I asked him, "If you could've avoided getting drafted and fighting in World War II, would you've taken the out?"

I was happy he answered seriously. "War is a suffering so powerful, it can destroy a man's soul. Sometimes I still hear that low, lamenting, lingering groan from a wounded soldier—a sliver burrowing under your skin that you can't squeeze out. It festers deeper and deeper until you're about to go mad."

He leaned forward on an armchair and drilled a hole in the area rug. "Everything in me would avoid it, but..." He touched his cross necklace. "The greatest gift God gives a man is letting him realize his helplessness. Too many fight it, distracting themselves from this truth. When you discover you're not indomitable, you can surrender and live."

A holy hush descended. I gazed at the ceiling, unsure what to say as memories of distracting myself with alcohol and women popped into my head. After a few minutes, he whispered, "And I wouldn't have had an excuse for not hearing Granny, right?"

During the war, Gramps got injured from shrapnel, losing hearing in his right ear. So, when Granny would say something he disliked, he'd shake his head, saying he couldn't understand her. She'd roll her eyes and accuse him of selective hearing.

I always admired how he loved Granny. Calling her his *war bride* even after sixty years of marriage and bragging about how she was still the most beautiful woman in the room.

Now, this morning as I sat in the solitude, I comprehended his advice. Through experiencing my parents' separation and my addiction journey, I discovered resilience, empathy, and trust. Realizing my helplessness, I relied on God, family, and community.

As the sun rose, I stopped journaling, grabbed my phone, and scrolled through photos from Michigan. The bare sugar maples standing tall in the dense woods, the javelin icicles hanging from the porch, and the doe digging its nose into the snow on the hill were my favorite nature shots from the trip.

I posted a few shots on social with the caption: Reminiscing about my white Christmas in Northern Michigan. Any guesses how I'm ringing in the new year? Hint: 📷 🥂 Check tomorrow for more clues.

Moriah called. "Hey, boss. Are you ready for today's wedding?"

"Think so. What are your plans tonight?"

"Still hanging out at a friend's, even though Pres helped plan it months ago."

As she talked about the activities they'd enjoy, I was happily surprised I didn't have any hard or numb feelings or disappointment toward Pres. We had a great run, but I needed to move on.

"Anyway, I called to see how you're doing," Moriah said.

"So, she informed you I broke it off, this time?" I asked.

"Yes, we talk or text every day. Just so you know, I think it was a good thing you called it off. Once she moved to Vegas, it was obvious you two were going in different directions."

I sighed. "Yep... so, you'll still work as my marketing guru?"

"You pay me too well."

"There you go..." Somehow talking to Moriah brought up lingering memories and questions about Presleigh and me.

"I hear that in your tone. What's bothering you?" Moriah asked.

"How Pres and I met seemed like a God move. We noticed each other immediately despite the crowd. I suppose it was just infatuation?"

"About that. I wanted to clear the confusion the day I returned the ring, but your mom showed up. And by the time I remembered to tell you, you two got back together. Then I assumed Pres explained it all but guess not."

"What?" I stood.

"Shortly after you hired me, I told her what a great boss you were. So, she thought you might be what she needed, meaning, someone different from Ciaran. She looked you up on your website and raved about how hot you were. She kept asking me to invite you to The Collective or to set you up. I hesitated to introduce you because you still weren't over Morgan. And honestly, Ciaran broke up with her just six months earlier, so she was still recovering. But I invited you to The Collective because I thought you'd benefit from the fellowship."

"Oh." Was I relieved Moriah cleared the confusion? Or disappointed Presleigh didn't tell me? How many times did I describe to Presleigh how our meeting was a divine setup? Why she didn't correct me, I didn't know, but she wasn't one to look back or indulge in introspection too much. She might've just thought it was irrelevant.

The important issue I needed to process was my desperation to get married. Since Presleigh was the healthiest girlfriend I've ever had, I was absolutely convinced she was the one. Therefore, I overlooked some pivotal issues. Now that I was thirty, I couldn't do *that* again.

But all wasn't lost. Because of her, I realized that the next time I'd commit to a serious relationship, I'd let it happen naturally. I wouldn't rush to the altar but keep my eyes wide open. I'd consult those I loved, stay open to the Holy Spirit's leading about our compatibility, and stick to my convictions about what I wanted in life.

And of course, I needed to heal from this relationship, especially how difficult the past month was on both my emotions and my self-confidence to discern what I wanted. For now, I'd just enjoy my singleness.

I'd also trust God to bring that woman in red to me. I was blown away by how timely the visions had come and the assurance they provided that I'd meet the love of my life someday.

After I got off the phone with Moriah, I deleted all the photos of Presleigh and me on my Instagram. Then I emailed Caroline and Uncle Erwin. "Sign me up for France this July." That would give me something to look forward to. The sun radiated a reddish-golden hue on the leaves of my Japanese maple.

Chapter 25
New Year's Eve night

As I pulled up to The Mayo, I was in a better place than the bridal session. I looked forward to shooting this wedding. How many opportunities did I have where I got paid to ring in the New Year?

The ceremony went without hiccups. I captured shots of the couple descending the imperial staircase as "Auld Lang Syne" played. Phil covered the guests tossing gold, black, and white confetti. As the couple reached the middle of the hall, glitter-filled white and gold balloons rained on them.

Phil and I accompanied the couple to the penthouse bar. After they toasted with Moscow mules, we went outside to the rooftop balcony. The couple rented a white LED love sign, and the decor team stationed it near the railing. It illuminated the balcony and cast a spotlight on the couple.

After we captured shots, the couple wanted a private moment. Grateful for the rest, especially as my ankle still hurt, I stood near the sign while they disappeared around the corner. Phil walked to the other end and took drone shots of the brightly lit skyline. The air was humid, making the slight breeze cooler on my face. Fortunately, my cream cable-knit sweater kept me warm.

As I looked beyond the skyline and toward the darkness, a neon yellow flash of lightning hit. *What the heck?* I grabbed my phone and looked up weather updates, but the app showed clear skies and temperatures in the forties.

"Excuse me," someone said.

I lifted my head and stared at the woman from two weeks ago, the one wearing Granny's bracelet. "Yes," I said, trying to remember her name... *Cheryl... Cindy... Celine... yes... Celine, that was it.*

I blinked as if transported to the Gilded Age. She wore an emerald, flowing gown that reminded me of what Granny wore in the framed picture. An emerald wrap covered Celine's shoulders and hung on the sides. She wore long white gloves, and on her left wrist, Granny's heirloom illuminated. Four strands of pearls with a multi-gem clasp of emeralds, sapphires, citrines, rubies, and diamonds. I was right.

"Are you taking pictures of guests in front of the sign?" she asked. When I noticed her before, I didn't consider her attractive...until now. With her dark brunette tresses styled in a short, angled bob, she resembled the transformed Audrey Hepburn in *Sabrina*.

I smiled. "What?"

"For us at the New Year's Eve party?" She played with her pearl drop earrings, which coordinated with a single strand pearl necklace.

"I can... but I'm shooting a wedding."

She winced. "I'm sorry. I assumed you were the hotel's photographer."

"I can snap a quick one," I said. "My couple is having a private moment."

"You don't mind?" Her breath circled like a cumulus cloud, floating toward me.

"No." How serendipitous, although if she was still with Jordan, I wasn't sure what could happen.

"I'll text my party." She grabbed her phone from a discreet pocket in her gown and texted. Then she looked at me. "I appreciate this," she said. "It's not every day I can wear my grandma's evening gown." She tugged the wrap tighter around her shoulders.

"It looks almost new."

The moonlight spotlighted her brown mole at the crease of her upper right lip. "I paid to have it treated."

I took a step toward her. "Do you like vintage clothing and jewelry?"

"Sometimes I wish I had lived in the thirties and forties. The ladies were elegant, my grandma especially."

"Is that why you like the bracelet?"

"One reason." She extended her hand, the gems winking at me, their rightful owner. I wanted to remove it from her wrist. *My precious.* "It was a gift from my boyfriend. It reminds me of my grandma. And..." Her fingers rolled the pearls on her necklace round and round.

"She and my grandpa died a year ago in a car accident. So, it feels like she's with me."

She had to go there. I took a step back.

"Sorry, I don't need to burden you with personal details," she said, cheeks turning slightly red.

"I lost my Granny five years ago, but it still seems like yesterday. Sorry about your grandma. Sounds like you two were close." I wanted to wrap my arms around her to comfort her as she stared at the ground.

"We were. We'd often come here for lunch. It meant the world to her when this hotel reopened."

"Same here." I nodded. "My granny insisted we attend the Grand Opening."

"Mine too! You were there?" She stepped closer. The crisp air merged with her peony perfume. It was a different fragrance than before, sweeter with a slight bergamot hue.

"Yep."

She tilted her head. "You look familiar."

"I was..." I wanted to explain how I was here asking her about the bracelet, but I didn't want to scare her away.

"I'm embarrassed..." She squinted. "You were shooting the bridal session a few weeks ago, right? You asked me about the bracelet?"

I nodded, relieved she remembered, so I could confirm the serial number. "Sorry if I acted like a stalker. It looks like my Granny's."

"I was preoccupied that day. There were many things converging at once, especially being at the hotel. My grandparents renewed their vows on the staircase landing..." She looked away then at me as she returned to rolling the strand of pearls. "I must've come across as self-absorbed."

The LED lights revealed her porcelain complexion. Her makeup was natural, showing off her oval face, high cheekbones, and almond eyes. I almost forgot about the heirloom; she looked angelic.

"There's no need to apologize," I said. "So, what was converging?"

"It was my last day at the ad agency where I was the assistant Creative Director. My boyfriend sent me enough clients, so I could work full time as a marketing consultant. Saying goodbye to my co-workers was more emotional than I had anticipated, not to mention being riddled with fear, leaving a great-paying job. And all on my birthday..." She took a step back. "I don't know why I'm opening up to you..."

Me either. But I liked it and wanted to learn more about her. "Cathartic, maybe?" I suggested. "I don't mind listening if it'll help."

"Well, it was special to have my first staycation with my boyfriend. He's been consumed with work. I wondered if he..." She waved her hand. "You don't want to hear that."

I smiled. I was curious about his angle. "You're good."

"It's not important. But he gifted his grandma's bracelet that night. Normally, he's not sentimental—he hardly talks about his family—so I was thrilled he trusted me with the heirloom."

I cringed, knowing he was deceiving her. It took all my self-control to not tell her the conversation I had overheard between him and his uncle. So, I dropped a hint, hoping she might put two and two together, realizing the truth. "I wanted my fiancée to wear my Granny's bracelet at our wedding." Ex-fiancée, but that didn't matter to her.

"That's romantic." Lights from the skyline illuminated her face. I wanted to capture a shot, but that might've broken the flow of our conversation. "My boyfriend shouldn't have shoved you like that, but he was afraid you'd hurt me or snatch the bracelet off my wrist. Obviously, you're a gentleman."

"I was shocked to see something resembling my granny's heirloom." I narrowed my gaze, hoping she'd take the hint.

"I bet. Once Jordan calmed down, he explained what happened. The designer probably made duplicates for clients. Someone saw it in the store's display or on a woman's wrist and requested the same or something similar."

"They have serial numbers." My judicial side wanted what was mine.

"Yes." She smiled, confident the heirloom on her wrist originally belonged to Jordan's grandmother. It wasn't arrogant, but slightly drawn to the right. She wasn't willing or ready to confirm my suspicions.

I grabbed my cell phone in my pants pocket, wanting to show her the serial number. But Dad's voice, in my paraphrase, echoed in my mind: *If you interfere with God redeeming the bracelet, it might delay the delivery.*

"Are you okay?" Celine took a step closer to me. The bracelet was within my reach.

"Yes..." I nodded. That brief pause knocked sense into me. Her face was soft and eyes ethereal; I couldn't call out Jordan. And she depended on him for her business. Lauren always accused me of being a bleeding heart. Fine, she was right.

"Garrett, are you ready?" Kaylie, the bride, approached.

"Yeah." I turned toward the bride quickly.

"Brad's using the restroom, but the wedding planner texted that cocktail hour is done, and dinner is about to be served," Kaylie said.

"I have to go," I said to Celine, then I turned to Kaylie. "Can this woman and her party take a few photos in front of your sign?"

Kaylie turned toward Celine. "I love your gown."

"Thank you. And yours is elegant—gives off vibes of old-world glam. Is it bespoke?" Celine asked.

Kaylie smiled. "It turned out better than I imagined... Regarding the sign, of course! Especially since you look like Grace Kelly."

Phil, holding the drone, appeared. "Headed to the reception?"

I turned to Celine and smiled. "Sorry, I don't have time to take the pictures but with smart phones, everyone's a photographer these days."

She waved her hand. "No problem. My party's in the bar, so who knows how long it would've taken for them to come out here."

"Good," I said, relieved she wasn't disappointed that I couldn't capture their picture. "Well, enjoy your night."

She smiled at me. "Appreciate it." Then she extended her hand to Kaylie. "Enjoy your wedding. And thank you for giving us permission to take pics in front of your sign. Once they join me, we won't take long."

"No problem. Take as long as you need." Kaylie winked.

As I carried Kaylie's train, Phil led the way as we walked through the penthouse bar. Jordan was chatting with a small group, his back facing us. I wanted to yank him by the collar and tell him he better treat Celine with care. But what good would that do?

Instead, we went to the elevators and waited on Brad. Celine strolled into the bar and approached Jordan. Shortly, he ushered her outside. What she saw in that dude was beyond me, but whatever.

Returning to the reception, I snapped shots of the couple's confetti-filled reception entrance and then their kiss at the sweetheart table. Fortunately, during the meal, we sat in the back, able to get off our feet and enjoy prime rib.

I kept thinking of Celine and the bracelet. A brick sat in my stomach. My heirloom was within my grasp. Yet, what if that bracelet she wore was a dupe?

Gramps said he had the bracelet custom made, so everything was symbolic of Granny. Pearls were her favorite gem. The four strands represented their four years apart. Emeralds were her favorite color; sapphires were his. The citrines illustrated his hope that one day, he'd return to marry her. The rubies signified his time in the war. The diamonds depicted endurance through suffering.

If she ever broke it off with Jordan, I could confirm the serial number. Would she return it? I needed to get her cell number just in case. I set my fork down, even though the prime rib melted in my mouth. This was urgent. "Phil, I'll be back in a few minutes. I've got to do something quick."

"I'll text if you need to get back," he said, slightly surprised.

"Thanks."

What would I say to Celine? *Hey, could I get your card? Why? Oh... for a marketing consult.*

I took the elevator to the sixteenth floor of the Crystal Ballroom, where they held the annual NYE soiree. As I exited the elevator, an acrylic sign "Royal Affair" on a gold stand welcomed me. That explained why Celine wore the vintage gown.

A staff member in a black jacket stood in front of the closed doors of the ballroom, hands behind her back like Secret Service.

"Ticket?" she said.

I pointed to the ballroom door. "Can I talk to a guest? They're asking if I'd take a few pictures. You can tell them Garrett Bettencourt is waiting. They're expecting me."

"Sorry, I need to see a ticket. You can text them yourself."

"I would, but they didn't bring their phone." I shook my head to emphasize the "problem" I faced. "They left it in their suite."

She remained stoic. "I'm sure if you wait here, they'll find you."

I took a step toward her, hoping to break her resolve. "Her name is Celine; he's Jordan."

"There are hundreds of guests here."

I received a text. "Hold on. Maybe they found someone else's phone."

It was Phil: Showtime! Hurry!

Coming, I texted and added a red-faced angry emoji.

A pet peeve was when the wedding party didn't allow us to get a break, especially to eat. Never mind that we worked nine hours on our feet or that our contract stated we would take a break during the meal.

I walked to the elevator. After the doors opened, Celine, arm in arm with Jordan, stepped out, followed by another couple. Jordan removed his hand off Celine's then chatted with the male guest.

I smiled at Celine. "Hi." I stepped toward her. "Here's my card. Do you have one for your marketing business? I might need some help."

I dipped into my black pants pocket to hand her the card, but Jordan stepped in front of us and took it.

"Get," he said.

"He's talking to me, Jordan," Celine said softly.

"I recognize you." Jordan's eyes grew almost ebony. He turned to the dude next to him. "This deadbeat was trying to pickpocket Celine's bracelet."

His friend glanced at me and shrugged.

Jordan looked at my business card. "You call yourself a photographer? Well, it doesn't cost much to make these flimsy cards online." He stuffed it in his breast jacket pocket.

"That's for Celine," I said, wanting to retrieve it from him. But now wasn't the time.

"Come on, baby." Jordan took her hand.

"Sorry," Celine mouthed.

After I stepped into the elevator, she turned and glanced at me. The doors closed.

At the reception, Phil asked where I'd been. The Dad, opening the evening with the father-of-the-bride speech, expected us to take photos.

After cutting the cake, Kaylie changed into a white crystal flapper dress. Perfect for their first dance, a choreographed Charleston. Phil and I captured great angles of the couple blitzing across the floor with their quick feet.

When midnight struck, guests, donning top hats and gold tiaras, shrilled and boomed with noisemakers. The groom dipped Kaylie then kissed her hard. I snapped pictures while trying to avoid getting trampled as guests crowded the couple. I earned my keep.

After shooting the sparkler exit at the front entrance, Phil and I were finished. So, once the couple returned to the Terrace Room, I said goodbye.

"This is our exit. I enjoyed shooting your wedding. And I'll text you a picture tomorrow."

"I can't wait to see it. And thank you for everything." Kaylie gave me a hug.

"Thanks, man." Brad shook my hand.

I looked around the room for Phil. Of course, the more social one, he stood near a table chatting with a guest. *Crap, he's my ride*. I texted him that I was headed to the rooftop balcony to cool off.

As I walked to the elevator, a golden cloud descended as the humidity grew. A red light flashed then faded. My hairs stood up and goosebumps appeared.

The woman in red with flowing blonde hair stood a foot away. The golden haze shrouded most of her face except her half smile and a round brown mole above her upper lip.

She lifted her hand toward me. The iridescent pearls on Granny's bracelet looked alive as they rotated around her wrist. The gemstones on the clasp shot beams of light. I stepped forward to touch her, but she disappeared as the elevator doors opened.

I'd enjoy meeting this woman in red, one day.

A Letter from the Author:

Thank you for reading *Christmas at Sonshine Barn*. I'm honored and humbled you invested your time journeying with Garrett. If you enjoyed this story, please leave me a quick rating on Amazon.

I enjoyed writing this adventure for many reasons, but a major one is personal: I was raised in the farmhouse where Garrett and his family celebrated Christmas. My parents converted our sprawling farm (outfitted with chickens, sheep, and steers) into a wedding venue called Sonshine Barn. I got married here in 2020.

Although the barn is closed during the frigid winters, the venue rents the farmhouse until the spring wedding season. Then, the farmhouse is exclusively available for the couple who books their wedding at the venue.

If you thought why "Son" and not "sun", that wasn't a typo. My parents gave the farm the moniker Sonshine Acres, reflecting Jesus as the Son of God and center of our lives.

Although I assigned Garrett to work as a wedding photographer before this novel, once I decided to feature him as the main protagonist in this installment, I knew the ideal place to send him. Northern Michigan is a hidden gem and often shocks visitors (like my husband) when they first visit this region. Gaylord is a tourist town off I-75, and you can drive that interstate up to the Upper Peninsula and all the way down to Florida. And Gaylord's alpine style is inspired by its sister city in Pontresina, Switzerland.

(In case you're wondering, I "featured" a fictional account of my parents in the Kayes who own the venue.)

Now, onto the cliff-hanger. Who is this woman in red?

If you haven't figured that out, read "Rescue in Amalfi", my

FREE short story I provide for my newsletter subscribers at SarahSoon.com. I have Easter eggs in there.

If you still aren't sure, I included the first chapter of *Love at the Mayo*, the next installment of the *Mayo Love* series.

LOVE AT THE MAYO

Excerpt

Chapter 1
May 5, 2018

I turned off the light in the living room of the condo. The only remaining trace of my presence was a note on his black hardwood desk.

Jordan,

I've moved out. We can arrange financial issues later.

He was on a two-week business trip to London, making it convenient for me to leave under the radar. I stepped into the complex's quiet hall with its staid grey walls and white with grey speckled marble floors. Why did I ever covet living here?

Waiting for the elevator, I held the last cardboard box of belongings. My diploma rested on top, since it wouldn't fit inside with my pictures, photo albums, and other keepsakes. *Please, get here elevator.*

The elevator doors opened, and Warner stepped out. Seriously! This past week, I'd come at ten until noon when Warner was golfing; otherwise, if he hadn't posed a threat, I would've just got everything out in a day, instead of in four.

He was a retired widower with time and money in abundance. He expended energy playing the town crier in the condo community. If anything happened in the building, he'd be the first to let everyone know, especially Jordan.

"Hi Celine," he said, blocking the entrance to the elevator. "Are you taking stuff to donate?"

He tilted his head, looking at the diploma. I lifted the box above his eyesight; he needed to mind his own business.

I smiled wide as if happy to run into him. "Yes, some clothes and shoes, but please step aside. I'm in a hurry."

Ignoring my request, he smiled. "You also graduated from TU? I'm surprised Jordan never told me. It's my alma mater." He pointed to the diploma.

"Yep." The elevator closed, but he didn't budge. I was stuck pretending to be cordial. *What was the universe trying to teach me?*

"No problem, but ..." He furled his brows. "You're not moving out, are you?" His voice was even keeled, revealing he asked out of curiosity, not concern.

"Oh..." I cleared my throat. "I found an office space to rent. So, I'm moving stuff in." I turned away not wanting him to see through my lie and tell Jordan.

"Where?"

My phone inside my purse rang. It was Dad, but I would've needed to drop the box to answer. "I've got to take this. I'll update you later," I said with more impatience than I intended, but I couldn't take his prying anymore.

He stepped aside, so I pushed the elevator's down button again. Fortunately, the door opened. I rushed inside and hit the closed button as Warner stared still wanting to converse. *Not today. Hopefully not ever.* When the doors closed, I leaned against the elevator wall. I'd call Dad from my car.

Once I was in the parking garage, I walked to Addy, my sedan. I stuffed the box into the crowded trunk, scooting a few items toward the back, so I could close it. Then I looked at the building.

Maybe I should remove the note and wait two weeks to call Jordan when he'd be at London's Heathrow Airport? No, that wouldn't do any good. He preferred working at the airport, loathing anyone bothering him with personal issues. I could text, asking him to call before he got home. That might work, depending on his mood. He'd hardly reached out since arriving to his destination, and when he did, it was all impersonal, either updating me about himself or asking about the condo, my work, and our friends. There was never a chance to talk about us. I wasn't surprised since lately, we became more like roommates than lovers.

Perhaps I could pick him up from the airport and break the news. How cold would that be? Whatever I did, I was screwed because there wasn't a convenient answer.

I only left the note because Dad and my best friend, Jennifer, insisted. They were afraid Jordan would talk me into staying. I argued that by telling him in person, he'd at least support my business. After all, I wouldn't stay now that he'd cheated on me. With my self-image at an all-time low, overly tired from packing, moving, and working, I caved in and left the note.

So, why was I standing here, questioning everything?

Dad called back. Maybe he could shed light on this conundrum.

"Hi." I wiped sweat off my forehead. Eighty-one degrees, and it was only May. We were in for a long, hot summer.

"Are you completely moved out?" His voice was riddled with angst.

"Yes, but..." I paused, so I wouldn't panic; otherwise, Dad might fly out here. "I ran into Warner just now, and he asked if I was moving. I was holding a box with my diploma on top."

"What did you say?"

"That I found an office space. But while that might prevent him from sounding an alarm with Jordan today, I'm concerned he'll text or call him within the week."

"I doubt he'd bother to text Jordan in London, but just wait until he returns."

"I don't want to chance it. I'm going to rip the note and just tell him in person—"

"No!" Dad interjected.

With my nerves already on edge, I jumped. I didn't expect him to yell. I scrambled into the car and slammed the door as if Addy could protect me from all the evils outside.

"We already went through this," he continued but in a slightly lower decibel.

"Hear me out," I said. "Warner catching me changes the game plan—"

"No, it doesn't. Just stick with the note."

"Nothing churns Jordan's temper worse than someone disrespecting him. If Warner inadvertently tips him that I moved out, Jordan will go Napoleon on me and declare war. No holds barred."

Dad immediately responded as if his quick release would defeat my arguments. "He will just because you broke it off and moved out. He doesn't want you to show him up. The guy's got an ego the size of Texas."

I covered my face, unsure what to do. As a marketing consultant, I depended on Jordan's referrals. He provided all but one of my clients, so the odds of them staying if Jordan advised them to find a different consultant weren't in my favor.

"Bottom line, I need to think about my business. After all, there's a chance he'll be relieved we're no longer going through the motions. If I can salvage our working partnership, I'll retain my clients. So, that's worth the risk of him dictating the parameters of the breakup." I didn't care that I was defending arguments I presented in an earlier discussion because I believed Dad wasn't realizing the implications yet. If he considered the run-in with Warner, he could hopefully see things clearer.

"If you're worried they'll jump ship, your maman and I want to invest in your business as you rebuild your clientele. Then you'd be completely cutting off all ties to Jordan."

"No, I have to do this myself." I groaned, tired of reinforcing my independence.

"You can come here for a while to clear the air. And we can figure out how to grow your business." Dad sounded hopeful and certain.

I closed my eyes, tempted to take him up on the offer. I could stay a month with them, living in The Villages, a retirement city in central Florida. It was created to make life convenient and fun, with each neighborhood having a pool and recreation center. They had three squares with restaurants, stores, and live entertainment every night. Who wouldn't want to live there and forget their troubles?

Jordan's voice rudely interjected in my mind. *You'll never reach your potential with your old man calling the shots.*

I opened my eyes. "I can't. I need to face him—"

"Absolutely not! Deal with the parasite through an attorney; otherwise, he'll bully you into submission."

"Stop yelling. Just stop! I can't." I gripped my head, feeling as though an invisible claw was squeezing my temples. I couldn't think clearly as he raised his voice, a trigger when I was with Jordan.

"I'm sorry," he said. A long pause. Dad was usually the voice of reason when tempers flared, but Jordan could burrow under his skin. "How about I fly there and help you?"

"Do we have to talk about this now?" I gripped the steering wheel. I worked hard at saving my money when I landed my first job. I wouldn't let Dad buy me a new car, so I drove an old clunker until I had enough to buy this gently used sedan with cash. It was worth all the beans and rice suppers at home, declining eating out with friends.

In hindsight, buying the car was an effort to celebrate having a career, not a means to enforce my independence. When I moved in with Jordan, he got irritated that I entrusted Dad to file my taxes. I argued that it saved me time while he enjoyed being helpful. Jordan said his accountant could file my taxes, so I pacified my "partner" because Jordan was my world, much to Dad's ire. This left me caught in the crossfires of their battle.

"When Jordan returns, we must be prepared for any scenario," Dad said in a moderate tone.

"He doesn't know where Jennifer lives," I said, paranoid about what Jordan might do.

"I'm talking about getting your down payment back."

"Oh." I was too consumed with moving out, I hadn't worried about the money.

"Is that Celine?" Maman's voice echoed faintly in the background.

"Hold on, Celine," Dad said. Then he sounded fainter as he addressed Maman. "Yes, I'm talking to her."

"Ask her to call me after you two are finished talking," Maman shouted wanting me to overhear.

"Sorry, she's eager to hear from you," Dad said, irritated. Maman had a habit of frequently interrupting conversations especially between Dad and me because she hated to miss anything. She was the social butterfly in our family.

"Can you fill her in? I'm not in the frame of mind to manage her twenty questions. And I need to get to Jennifer's, take a shower, and plan my week." My chest burned, but I'd run out of antacids in my purse.

"Sure, but please text her. She's concerned."

I groaned. "In an hour maybe."

"Remind me. When does Jordan return?" Dad asked.

"The seventeenth." I loathed uncertainty and chaos, which was why I worked hard to be scheduled, organized, and punctual. And why I was first attracted to Jordan. He liked life controlled and perfect. But nothing was in order now. So, how bad could it get when he'd find the note? Anytime, I thought about the seventeenth, my mind would blank.

"Good. That gives us time to come up with a game plan... Celine? Did we get disconnected?"

"Sorry," I said, returning to consciousness. "Can we wait until Jordan returns?"

"You might as well concede the fight. We've got to be three steps ahead."

"The receptionist could take over payments since she's already made moves on him," I said, wanting to blame her.

"Nor does he want to lose control over you, so it's more than just the money."

"No, it's all about greed. He doesn't want to part with tens of thousands of dollars. You have no idea how obsessed he is about joining the millionaire's club."

"That's why you must work through an attorney—"

"I'm removing the note and will call him in person, but I'll go tomorrow to avoid an interrogation with Warner."

"Celine Elizabeth!" Dad's voice was louder than ever. "Drive to Jennifer's and forget about telling him in person..." He paused, probably to regain his composure. "I promise I won't fly out there until you ask, nor will we invest in your business if you don't want us to. But just leave the note."

I'd take the deal for now. "Alright. Look, I'm headed to Jennifer's, so I'm going to hang up."

After I got off the phone, I pulled onto the street and briefly glanced at the twenty-story condo building, mostly glass and steel with tan bricks set in the middle. But it no longer seemed modern or upscale, just frigid and bland. The traffic was slow, so I took my time leaving.

It took me about fifteen minutes longer than usual to get to Jennifer's. I drove about twenty to thirty miles an hour, stopping at the yellow lights (earning some honks and birds in the process), and re-routed a few times when I turned onto the wrong streets. Although the day was sunny with a few clouds, my mind lay wrapped in a thick fog.

Damn! I drove past the street to Jennifer's. Blood rushed to my head. Only a few blocks down, in a seedy part of town, was the Mexican restaurant where I caught Jordan and the receptionist holding hands. At first, I wasn't sure if I was more shocked at seeing them together or that he was patronizing this hole-in-the-wall. But now, I couldn't get out of my mind how easily he replaced me. So, today, I wasn't ready to glance at that place again. I turned into a parking lot to get back on the road, heading north.

Once I pulled into the right street, I exhaled. Jennifer's condo complex contained five buildings, each with four, two story-units. They featured an all powder-blue exterior with white shutters, like what you'd see on a hill overlooking the Mediterranean.

I rested my head on the steering wheel. Although I'd physically left Jordan, what if it took months or years before I was completely free?

*

---

* Do you want to read Love at the Mayo once it's released? (Yes, Celine's path intersects with Garrett's.) Subscribe to my author newsletter, so you can get notified when it's available for preorder.

Acknowledgements

It takes a village to write a book, and my village could be a city.

Huge shout-out to my beta readers, Mari Eygabroad, Karen Grunst, Laurie Salvacion, and Janet Weiner, for your helpful feedback.

I'm grateful to those serving as reviewers. Thanks Kristi Bridges, David Crawford, Mari Eygabroad, and Becky Green for submitting edits based on your Advanced Reader Copy.

Thanks to my fellow Lady Lits: Mari Eygabroad, Susan Marie Graham, Cindy Godwin, Linda Sammaritan, Janet Weiner, J. Bea Wilson, and Nancy Ness, the founder of our group. We've become a sisterhood of writers within a short period. I've gleaned from all of you!

Appreciation goes to *Unbreakable Spines*, a local critique group. You've welcomed this contemporary fiction writer to your heavily dominated sci-fi and fantasy stories. Shout out to Meg Perdue, a member of this group, for meeting with me weekly to critique our works. You've helped me sharpen my writing skills. Also, through *Unbreakable Spines*, I connected with Michele Chiappetta who co-founded the group. She's the brilliant editor of this story. Check out her services at Two Birds Author Services.

I appreciate Story Grid, an online writing course, for honing my storytelling craft. I used the tools the course provided to help strengthen this novel. And shout out to the members of the Story Grid cohort group for helping me to better understand the concepts Story Grid teaches.

Thank you to Aaron Pegg and Curt Cowgill for giving photography feedback. Your insights were helpful! And thanks to Seth Barnett for serving as a photography consultant on the project. You provided the technical knowledge the story needed.

Thanks to April Auld, Sarah Freeman, Andrea Moniz,

and Mary Tomaski for providing helpful information about addiction.

Speaking of Sarah, I'm grateful for your photography services for the book cover. You went above and beyond, capturing several shots of the farmhouse and venue.

Thanks to Greg Kates for the invaluable information about police procedures.

I appreciate Bruce and Barb Brown at Alpine Chocolat Haus for reviewing Chapter 15 for accuracy about your chocolate shop!

To all my family (the Freeman and Ward sides) thank you for your love and support. I'm grateful for your going on this journey with me.

To my husband, you've worn many hats helping me as I wrote this story. I appreciate you critiquing the manuscript, especially making sure it was coming from a male point of view, and your cooking and cleaning when I was working long hours to meet a deadline. I love you!

And to my Father who's directed my life including my writing journey. You're my "agent" leading me through with patience, wisdom, and peace. This book wouldn't have gotten published without your divine leading!

About the Author

Although *Christmas at Sonshine Barn* is Sarah's debut novel, she's helped authors share their stories. She collaborated in a devotional anthology, *Option Ocean,* ghostwritten two memoirs, and written magazine articles for *Tulsa Lifestyle Magazine.* She's also edited non-fiction books ranging from medical topics to Christian living.

Now, she writes transformative fiction where characters experience inner healing, so they can find love and renew their faith. *Christmas at Sonshine Barn* inaugurates the contemporary romance series called Mayo Love. This series centers around two protagonists who undergo transformation and find love.

Sarah and her husband reside in Oklahoma. You can find her at: Sarahsoon.com.

Facebook: @SarahSoonWriter

Instagram: @sarahsoon38

Goodreads: SarahSoon

Made in the USA
Monee, IL
14 December 2024